REUNITED WITH HIS RUNAWAY BRIDE

BY
ROBIN GIANNA

MILLS
BOON

Published in Great Britain 2016
By Mills & Boon, an imprint of HarperCollins*Publishers*
1 London Bridge Street, London, SE1 9GF

© 2016 Robin Gianakopoulos

ISBN: 978-0-263-06532-9

After completing a degree in journalism, then working in advertising and mothering her kids, **Robin Gianna** had what she calls her 'awakening'. She decided she wanted to write the kind of romance novels she'd loved since her teens, and now enjoys pushing her characters towards their own happily-ever-afters. When she's not writing, Robin's life is filled with a happily messy kitchen, a needy garden, a wonderful husband, three great kids, a drooling bulldog and one grouchy Siamese cat.

Visit the Author Profile page at millsandboon.co.uk for more titles.

Sibling relationships are unique and special, and I'd like to dedicate this book to my brother's memory. Mark, I have a feeling a few of the stars in the sky are really you, lighting the firecrackers you loved to throw at me while the other angels laugh at your jokes. I miss you.

Praise for
Robin Gianna

CHAPTER ONE

"You know, that tummy of yours isn't what you can call a 'baby bump' anymore. More like a baby beach ball," Bree Donovan teased. She glanced at her friend Emma, who was settling herself in the passenger seat of her car. "Good thing he didn't decide to pop out while you were flying over the mountains. Giving birth on a plane would be a little stressful, don't you think?"

Bree had to at least lightly chide her friend for waiting to travel until she was thirty-seven weeks along in her pregnancy, after she'd told Emma more than once she shouldn't. Not that the woman ever listened to advice, and in fact usually did the opposite of anything suggested to her.

"I know you wanted me to come sooner, but I wasn't ready to deal with Sean yet," Emma said with a grimace. "Lecturing me and fussing over me like I'm still a little kid instead of twenty-nine years old. Besides, the reason I look like I swallowed a volleyball is because the baby is still high and happy, with no intention of coming soon, I'm told."

And even if she hadn't been sure of that, free-spirited Emma probably wouldn't have worried about it anyway, would she? Bree would have smiled, remembering the way Sean alternately rebuked then pampered his sister, if it didn't make her heart hurt thinking about Sean at all.

Though not thinking about him had become impossible with Emma coming back to San Diego for a while.

The ache in her chest was joined by self-mockery. Who was she kidding? It didn't matter that she and Sean had broken up six miserable months ago—he was on her mind way too often, anyway. It also didn't matter that their relationship had started to list toward rocky shore shortly after their engagement, showing how wrong she'd been during those first starry-eyed months with him. Obvious, important differences had wedged between them, slowly shaking the foundation of what had seemed like perfection together. How that had happened was something she still couldn't figure out—didn't falling in love at nearly first sight mean it was meant to be?

The blinding happiness she'd felt then had convinced her it did. And was *blinding* the right word, or what? She'd certainly chosen not to open her eyes to all the reasons things could never work out between the two of them until after he'd put a ring on her finger, making their breakup all that much harder for both of them.

"Oh, and speaking of Sean," Emma said, emphasizing her brother's name in a way that had Bree bracing herself for what might be coming next, "I wanted to confess something."

"Confess what?"

"Mom told me he's been gloomy and restless ever since you two broke up. So I set him up with a dating service to help him move on. Just so you know, in case you see him on a date."

"You did what?" Bree's mouth fell open and she stared at her friend.

"You don't mind, do you?" Emma raised her eyebrows, the picture of surprised innocence. "I'm just trying to help him find someone better suited to him, and he works so much, he doesn't have time to meet women. I mean, you're the one who broke the engagement. And are ready to move to Hawaii. Right?"

Cold, shocked dismay shot through Bree at Emma's statement. Why, she didn't know. She shouldn't care one bit. A rational woman wouldn't. It was over between them for a lot of good reasons, and she was moving on, literally and figuratively.

"Of course I don't mind." And she didn't. And maybe her nose was growing, because the thought of seeing Sean with another woman on his arm, thinking of him sleeping with someone else, made her feel sick to her stomach.

"I figured you'd want him to move on," Emma said with a nod. "You probably know how close he and Dad were. When Dad was so sick in hospice, he told Sean one of the things he hated most about being sick was that he wouldn't get to see our kids when we had them, and told both of us he knew we'd be great parents. Made Sean promise to live his own life to the fullest, the way he had. It…it makes me really sad, you know?"

"I'm sorry." Bree reached to squeeze Emma's knee. "That has to feel horrible, with your little one on the way now."

"It breaks my heart that my baby's never going to

know his grandpa. And after Dad died, Sean was even more determined to be the man Dad raised him to be." Emma's eyes filled with tears. "Wants to be just like him, you know? A good doctor, a loving husband and the world's best father."

Bree's throat closed, and she couldn't think of a thing to say in response. How much Sean wanted a family of his own had become painfully, fatally clear, but she hadn't realized until this moment how much that desire was tied up with his love for his dad, and his mother, too. Bree might not know anything about having the world's best father, but she did know with certainty that Sean would be amazing at all those things, even though she couldn't be a part of it. "I wish I'd known your dad."

"Me, too. He was special." A deep sigh left Emma's chest. "So that's part of the reason Sean was so happy to think he was going to be settling down with you and eventually having a family. Since that didn't...turn out so well, I want to help him find that. Be happy again. I'm not sure he's gone on any dates yet, so I'm going to be nagging him about it."

Bree wanted to say, *Well, thanks a lot for that, you traitor*, but knew that would sound ridiculous and awful, under the circumstances.

She drew a long, slow breath. There didn't seem to be much else to say on that depressing subject, and she forced a teasing tone to change it. "Think that volleyball belly will make you feel right at home on the beach?" She knew the game had been one of Emma's favorite pastimes and wanted to steer the conversation somewhere light, away from distressing thoughts of Emma's dad, and of Sean and their spectacular breakup. Away from visions of him with other women that dredged up memories and emotions better left deeply buried.

"Yeah. Except I'll be the proverbial beached whale on the sidelines, not a player," Emma said, smiling again. "Don't tell Sean, but I admit being home always makes me feel good. It'll help me get back into shape in no time. With the bike path on the bay right outside Sean's place and not too far from Mom's, I'll be able to easily run with a stroller."

Bree opened her mouth to say she'd love to join her, then shut it again. It seemed impossible that she'd be moving in just over a week, and she couldn't deny that a part of her kept thinking about how things might have been different.

Over and done with. In the past, and her new job would be a step up. Right? It would.

Maybe her expression was saying something she didn't want it to, because Emma tipped her head. "You really have to move to Honolulu? I mean, now? I wish you could be here when the baby's born."

"I wish I could be, too. But they need me to start soon because an ER doc is leaving. And it's a good opportunity."

"Not sure I believe it could be any better than here."

"It's a university Level One Trauma hospital," Bree said. "With a chance to move into the emergency department director's position at some point. Plus you know it's important to me to take part in the bigger surf competitions. Living in Hawaii will make that easier."

"Hmm. I suppose. Though you managed to do that living in San Diego." Emma raised one eyebrow. "Truth. Are you moving because of Sean?"

"Of course not. We found out we're not right for one another before we made the mistake of making it permanent. It's a good thing." Not that it had felt very good at the time, but she'd managed to move on. Pretty much.

"And all those reasons you came up with for it not working out between you two are a crock, if you ask me. So he likes to be in charge and is used to taking care of people, and you don't need taking care of. So, what? Your independence is one of the things he loved about you, even if he wouldn't admit it."

"I don't think so. It was one of the things about me that bugged him."

"Wrong, and I know so." Emma folded her arms across her chest, and Bree could feel her staring hard at her. "Another thing Dad said to Sean before he died? He asked him to take care of me and Mom. Yeah, that's sexist, but he loved us and worried how it would be without him. And Sean was about as rock solid a support as a person can be for us, even when he got aggravated with me. Who in their right mind doesn't want a guy who cares about you that way?"

"You, for one." Bree stared in disbelief before turning back to the road. "You've bitterly complained about Sean wanting to take care of you, badgering you instead of letting you live your life the way you want to."

"He's my brother, not my boyfriend. So maybe he did a little too much trying to take Dad's place, but, even when it made me mad, I always knew it was because he loves me. There's such a thing as being independent to a fault, you know." Her hand waved around dismissively. "And part of the breakup being because you wanted to run off and elope when he wanted a big wedding with all our extended family here, and all the cousins and kids dancing and everyone having fun? Plain stupid. Don't tell me you two couldn't have figured out a way around that."

"You're forgetting even bigger things," Bree said. Why were they hashing over all this again? Probably because she and Emma hadn't talked about it since she and Sean had first broken up, and one more round of torture was inevitable. "I wanted a no-care condo so we could be free to go to surf competitions and all the other traveling I need to do, and he wanted a bigger house with a yard, a cat and a dog tying us down."

And kids. The biggest thing of all. The one thing there was no way to compromise about.

"I know being independent is important to you. I get that having pets and children would make that harder. But maybe as time went on, you'd feel differently. Haven't I had to do things differently than I thought? Move back home for a while, when I never thought I'd do that?" Her hands cupped her belly in a gesture filled with tenderness. "My baby wasn't planned," she said softly. "But I can tell you I'd do anything for him, and he's not even here yet. So tell me why you're so sure you don't want kids."

"Let's just say my family dynamics and relationships with my parents convinced me." It was past time to change the subject, but before she could say anything more, a monstrous delivery truck moved into her peripheral vision, running through the red light into the intersection, straight toward Emma's side of the car.

"Hang on!" she yelled, her heart doing triple time as

she swerved into what little space seemed free. Inches between her lane and the one filled with oncoming traffic. Got half a car length between them and the truck. Saw it bearing down on them, behind Emma now. But not far enough. In what seemed like bizarrely slow motion, she watched it slam into the back-seat door with a bone-jarring impact. Shoved them into the next lane of cars with another deafening screech of metal.

Emma's screams tore through Bree's very soul. Then it was dark.

"Which room? Is it ready?" Bree ran through the ambulance entry of the ER, hanging on to the gurney carrying Emma that was being steered by two of the EMTs who'd responded to the accident. Clutching the bar like a lifeline, as though if she just held on tight enough, Emma would be okay.

"Which room?" she repeated hoarsely. Bree's throat felt so dry and tight she was surprised she'd managed to get a single word out, but even one second of time lost might be too much.

"Trauma Two!" a nurse shouted back.

Bree pivoted that direction along with the gurney, using her free hand to swipe at the blood dripping into her eye. She scrubbed her hand down the side of what had been a new blue dress, but her clothes and her own injuries were last on her list of things to care about. There was no doubt Emma had suffered some serious injuries, and being conscious and lucid now didn't mean that couldn't change in a single heartbeat.

As the gurney swung into Trauma Two, she could see Dr. Kurz was already there, gowned and waiting for his patient, and she was beyond thankful for that. "Okay, Emma," she said, letting go of the railing to reach for her friend's hand. "We're here now and everybody's ready to help you."

"Bree?" Emma's dark eyes, filled with fear, stared up at her from the gurney, her voice a muffled whisper through her oxygen mask. "It hurts. It…it hurts so much."

"I know, sweetie. Hang in there," she said, shoving down the fear that had filled her throat the second she'd awakened from the knock on her head to see Emma trapped and unconscious. She swallowed hard. Was there something, anything, Bree could have done to prevent the accident?

She lifted a shaking hand to wipe away the blood trickling into her eye again. *Please, please let them be okay.*

The medics, as breathless as Bree, started in with their rapid-fire report to everyone in the room. "Twenty-nine-year-old, thirty-seven weeks pregnant. Vehicle struck by a truck, passenger side, pushing vehicle into oncoming traffic. Extensive damage to multiple vehicles. Forty-five-minute extraction, GCS fifteen, last heart rate one thirty-five, BP eighty over fifty."

Bree blinked fiercely as she listened. Remembered. The impact had nearly flipped Bree's car as it skidded into a sedan coming the opposite direction. The horrific shriek of tearing, crumpling metal. Her own door caving in, knocking her head against the window as the air bag exploded into her face, briefly blinding her as she heard Emma's screams just before Bree blacked out for a moment. Awakening to turn, stunned and disoriented. Seeing Emma's body terrifyingly still and bleeding.

"Were you the driver of the car, Dr. Donovan?" Kurz asked, looking at her more closely than she wished he would.

"Yes." She should have known he'd figure that out, but her own minor injuries weren't an issue at the moment, and she was more than capable of helping the team. "But I'm fine."

Kurz gave her a nod. "Let's get the patient moved over."

Hearing the senior critical care doc's calm, commanding voice helped her focus as she watched four pairs of hands lift the board Emma was strapped to, sliding her onto the trauma bed. Bree took her place at Emma's right as the team cut away her clothes.

"That's about the only top that fits me now," Emma gasped through her oxygen mask.

"I'm sorry, but we have to," she soothed, swallowing hard. As though her blouse mattered one iota under the circumstances. She stroked Emma's hair then reached to squeeze her hand. Could she hope it was a good sign Emma had even thought about it? "I'll get you another just as pretty, I promise."

In mere seconds, the team had Emma set up with blood-pressure cuff, IV, and cardiac leads to the monitor as the surgical resident examined every inch of her, and Bree was so thankful again that they weren't in that smashed car anymore, or the ambulance, as good as the EMTs had been, but finally here, getting Emma the help she needed.

"Tell us where you're hurting," Kurz said as the X-ray tech got ready to shoot films.

"My chest, my stomach." Emma moaned. "My arm and leg. My baby—oh, please make sure my baby—"

"I promise everyone's going to take good care of the baby, Emma," Bree managed to say. Question was, would it be too late? "Let's get a monitor on him, check how he's doing."

A nurse got the monitor on Emma's belly. The infant's heartbeat showed up strong and steady, and relief made Bree's knees so wobbly, she gripped the side of the bed to hold herself up. Whether he was ready or not, baby had to come into the world soon, in case he or Emma took a turn for the worse.

It took every ounce of restraint Bree could muster to just stand there and watch the team work instead of assisting in some way. But right now, she had to remember her training as an ER physician who was used to trauma just like this and let the team do their job. Pretend the woman on this bed wasn't her close friend. Wasn't the sister of the man she'd been in love with not so long ago, no matter how unsuited they'd proved to be for one another.

Thinking of him and how devastated he'd be by this accident ratcheted her adrenaline even higher. Had her chest tightening at the thought that he might blame Bree, and maybe she deserved it. "Anyone know if Dr. Sean Latham is in the hospital? This is his sister. He needs to be notified right away."

Kurz's attention swung to her in surprise before he barked more orders.

Bree closed her eyes, thinking of Sean hearing the

overhead paging him to Trauma Two. He'd be so unprepared for what he was about to walk into. Sean got frustrated with Emma sometimes, but he adored his little sister.

Bree glanced at Emma's monitor and her stomach lurched. "Heart rate's one-sixty."

"Blood pressure's dropping, too," a nurse said.

Kurz had his stethoscope and fingers on Emma's poor, bruised chest. "Hemothorax. Hold on X-ray. We need the chest tube tray—you got this?" he asked the surgical resident.

Bree didn't like the shaky affirmative of the resident's answer, and anxiety rose in her own chest as she prayed the resident had the confidence and experience to get the tube inserted into Emma's lung fast. Steadily stroking Emma's hair, she couldn't say for sure if she was trying to calm Emma or herself.

Kurz continued barking orders, sending techs and nurses scurrying. "I want Anesthesia down here now, and why the hell isn't OB here yet? And get the NICU team."

"Bree, what's happening? NICU team?" Emma's eyes were wide and scared, and Bree took her hand and squeezed it gently.

"Got to get you fixed up and deliver the baby. You're going to meet your little guy today. Can you believe it?" Somehow, she managed to keep her tone light. "You still going to go with the name you told me you'd decided on?"

"What? I'm not ready! I—"

"We're going to help you be ready. It's going to be okay."

"I… Bree," Emma whispered, her words slurring. "I feel…funny. It's… Is it getting dark? Where…?"

Just like that, Bree saw her eyes close, her head go limp and her skin turn as white as pure, pearly beach sand.

"Emma!" *Oh, no. Please, no.* "Emma, stay with me!" Her shouts were punctuated by the cardiac monitor alarm, heart rate forty, thirty, fifteen, then asystole. Flat line. The sight of that neon line felt like a sharp knife blade slicing right through Bree's heart as the screech of the monitor filled her ears. Air didn't seem to be getting to her lungs. Watching hands pumping on Emma's chest, hearing Kurz's voice demanding Epi and oxygen, felt utterly surreal.

"What the…?"

Bree whirled. Sean. Standing there in the doorway, staring at his sister in shock.

"Pulmonary injury. Right hemothorax." It was hard to choke out the words, and the next were even harder. "Coded twenty seconds ago."

"About to place a chest tube," Kurz said as he worked. "We're going to OR Three. When we can get her there."

Before one more second ticked by, Sean moved into action. He shouldered the surgery resident aside to get the tube placed as quickly and efficiently as possible. Immediately the blood began to flow, releasing the pressure on her lungs and heart.

Bree watched him secure the tube to the chest wall when the startling beep of the cardiac monitor cut through the fog in her brain. *Emma's heart's back! She's back!* But each beat was so far apart. Slow. Too slow. She must have some other serious injury. Needed more blood circulating. Needed for her heart to pump harder. Needed it for both her and her baby.

Bree knew what had to be done and drew on reserved strength to get the words out. "We have to take the baby."

"Not yet," Sean said, a tortured fierceness on his face she'd seen only once before—the day they'd broken up. "Is OB on the way? We can wait till then."

"We can't wait. We have to do it now or we'll lose both of them." She hated that her last words came out in a near sob. How emotional. How unprofessional. But Emma was her friend, and for a split second Bree had seen the overwhelming love in her eyes as she'd cupped her belly, so happy to soon be holding her baby in her arms. If they couldn't save Emma, they could at least save one life. Bring this precious baby, a part of her, into the world.

"A few more minutes. Emma's got a strong heart. She—"

"Dr. Donovan is right," Kurz said. "You take over chest compressions while we do a crash and burn C-section to get the baby."

"I'll do the prep and assist," Bree said as she snapped on gloves. For Emma. For Sean. For the baby who might never know his mother.

Kurz nodded and Sean opened his mouth to argue more, but the look on Kurz's face was clear, and, as he was senior ED doc running the code, the call was his to make. Wordlessly, Sean took over compressions, rhythmically pushing on his sister's chest. As she saw the mix of determination and anguish on his face, Bree's heart cracked.

"You ready?" Kurz asked Bree as she quickly swabbed Emma's belly with antiseptic.

"Ready." It wasn't true, she wasn't ready for them to bring this baby into the world without his mother, but it had to be done. Saving this child was at least one thing she could do to try to make up in some tiny way for driving her car into harm's way.

Barely aware of a different nurse rolling a warming cart next to her, Bree handed Kurz the scalpel and watched as he made a full, midline incision as fast as he could. They delivered the baby and suddenly the NICU team was right there, swooping in to grab the baby up, leaving Kurz to refocus on Emma. Numb, Bree kept glancing over to watch them give the infant chest compressions and oxygen before rubbing him all over to stimulate him. Surreal that, at the very same time, Sean and the team were insistently working on the baby's mother in nearly the same way.

It seemed to go on so long with no response at all from the tiny boy, she started to lose hope. She glanced up at Sean, who was still doing strong, unrelenting chest compressions on his sister. Emma's heart rate had dropped to barely a blip on the screen. But Sean was still determined. Still believing.

Losing both of them would take a terrible toll on the man so close and connected to his family. Hadn't they already lost the father they'd dearly loved? She tried to swallow down the deep pain choking her when she thought she heard a weak cry that sent her attention flying to the NICU team and the baby. Her heart lifted, soared, when his cries strengthened. His deep purple color lightened and slowly pinked up.

Her gaze moved back to Sean, who was looking at the baby while still performing steady chest compressions. Awe slid across his face, mingling with that fierceness as their eyes met. Her throat closed when, even in the midst of his intense work trying to resuscitate Emma, he gave Bree a quick, nodding salute.

Bittersweet emotion tangled around her heart as the team placed the infant in the warming cart and took off with him, doubtless heading to the NICU to be stabilized and evaluated. Tears stung Bree's eyes as they met Sean's, and she prayed again that the baby would be okay. That Emma would still, somehow, survive. That she'd be here to hold her infant son in her arms.

Seeing Bree's beautiful green eyes fill with tears made Sean somehow even more determined to save his sister's life. As though he weren't already giving it everything he had in him to make that happen.

His mother had already been through too much tragedy. And if Emma died? He knew that blow would practically kill his mom, too. And not only did Emma have a lot of living yet to do and a child to raise, he was not going to have Bree feeling some kind of lifelong guilt because the two of them had obviously been in that car crash together. Most likely she'd been driving, but she was so good behind the wheel, he knew it couldn't have been her fault.

For all those reasons, his sister was going to live. That was all there was to it.

"Sean." Kurz reached to touch his shoulder, and he knew what was coming. "I'll take over."

"No. Keep up with the epinephrine and blood transfusion for another minute. I'm not being crazy. I'm going to make this happen. She—"

"Sean." Bree's tone of voice was completely different than Kurz's had been. Held a tentative, then rising excitement. "Sean, you did it! Heart rate's…heart rate is rising to…eighty!"

He glanced at the monitor. What he saw there nearly made him fall over, as though he could feel the world slowly turning on its axis. Emma's heart was in normal sinus rhythm, etched on the screen in steady, perfect, neon green spikes. For real.

His whole body started to shake. "Notify the other surgeon on call and any GYN available," he somehow managed to croak out. "Get her to the OR to figure out what all's going on."

Everyone moved into action. Sean stood there motionless, because at that moment moving a single muscle felt impossible. He watched them roll his sister from the room, the terrifying details of her bruised and battered body seared into his brain. He looked down at his hands, Emma's blood still covering them from when he'd inserted the tube, and didn't want to think about how close he'd come to losing her.

How he still might.

Somehow, he moved toward the sink, feeling as if every bit of support in his legs had disappeared. Kurz must have realized he didn't feel like talking. Just clasped his shoulder in a tight grip for a lingering moment before he left the room. A smaller hand pressed against his back, and he didn't have to turn to know it was Bree.

For a lot of reasons, he didn't want to talk to her, either. The adrenaline—and, yes, the terror—of the past twenty minutes was leaching from his body pretty fast, leaving behind a mental and emotional shakiness and upheaval he didn't want to admit to, or show, to anyone. Least of all her, the woman who'd left him with plenty of the same kinds of disturbing feelings to deal with for the past six months.

"Tough day," Bree whispered.

Tough? The way she said the word had him realizing how tough it must have been for her, too. In the middle of the crisis, he hadn't been able to process that. Tough to be in what must have been one horrific crash. Tough to go through whatever had happened at the scene after. Tough to see Emma code, and, despite all that, step up and help bring her baby into the world without a second of hesitation.

Iciness crept through his veins as the full reality hit him in the gut, knocking what wind he had left right out again. Bree had been in that car, too. Tough? The word didn't exist that could describe how he'd have felt if Bree had been seriously injured in that accident as well. It didn't matter that she wasn't a part of his life anymore. Then as soon as that thought came, he knew that was only partly true.

It mattered because she'd be a part of him forever.

He turned, and her soft hand moved to his arm. He rested his palm on top of it, and that simple connection somehow soothed the raw chaos burning in his chest.

"Even tougher day for you, I'm guessing. You okay?"

"Okay. I'm…I'm so sorry."

"Sorry?" Was she blaming herself after all?

"I was driving. It technically wasn't my fault, but…

you know. I have to wonder if I could have prevented it somehow."

"No, you don't. Because I'm not wondering, and I'm sure Emma isn't either. You may be a hellion on wheels, but you're a damned good hellion. Always beyond alert behind the wheel, and I've never once seen you cross the safety line."

"Thank you. I think." A tiny, wobbly smile touched her lips, despite the tears swimming in her eyes. "Obviously, we both know Emma's not out of the woods yet. But she sure showed she's one resilient woman, didn't she?"

"Yeah." They hadn't even learned, yet, the full extent of her injuries. Who knew what it would take for her to recover? "But somehow, I know she's going to be all right. Even if that sounds stupid." Maybe it was some mysterious, brother/sister connection, but from the second he'd tried to bring her back, he'd known it wasn't over. Known with utter certainty that he'd get to see her again. A little like he'd known when their dad had finally given in to the cancer he'd fought for so long.

"Doesn't sound stupid. I may not have a sibling, but I've heard plenty of stories. There seems to be some sort of ESP about one another." The green eyes staring into his were deeply serious. Questioning. Hopeful. "I don't suppose that ESP extends to the baby?"

"No gut feeling about the baby, unfortunately." A baby he'd been upset with Emma about, wondering how his little sister had gotten herself pregnant without a husband, and even angrier that she stubbornly refused to say who the father was. But the deep, wrenching grief he'd felt when he'd first seen the baby, blue and seemingly lifeless in Bree's remarkably steady hands when she'd delivered him, had made him realize with a shock that he already felt a connection to the little guy in spite of all that.

Which had him wondering about the same question he'd asked a hundred times. How was it possible that Bree didn't want that kind of connection someday with a child of her own?

Everything in him seemed to squeeze until he couldn't breathe. Since he didn't know how to manage the band of emotions strangling him, he forced himself to ease away from Bree, not wanting to think about all that. About her relationship with Emma, about how and why his life and Bree's had gotten tangled up then ripped apart. About the day his sister had introduced her freshman dormitory roommate to him, insisting they should meet after Bree had moved to San Diego to work in the same hospital he did.

His first sight of her was still branded into his brain. He knew it would be branded there forever.

She'd stood silhouetted in his doorway wearing a pale yellow sundress. Tall and proud, lean and fit. Backlit by the bright, Southern California sunshine, a confident smile tipping the corners of her beautiful lips. Her lively, intelligent eyes had met his and held—eyes that were such a mesmerizing sea green he'd almost forgotten how to breathe. Her thick, shining hair, a color somewhere between golden honey and liquid fire, had skimmed her tanned, bare shoulders, and he'd had to stop himself from reaching out to see which was softer—those silken strands or her smooth skin.

He'd never believed in love at first sight. Who did something so stupid as that? Who let themselves fall in love because of hormones or lust or chemistry, and not because that woman and you were truly compatible? Not concerned with whether or not they shared a mutual vision of the future? Whether or not that person might break your heart?

Who did that? Him, apparently, and he had the deep scars on that vital organ to prove it.

Bree's nearness, the caring softness in her eyes, made him really look at her. Made him take in the sight of her beautiful face marred by disturbing swelling, scrapes and blood. Those physical reminders of how easily she could have been even more badly hurt, or worse, made his throat close and his gut clench. Had him wanting to pull her close, wanting to take care of her.

Wanting to never let her go.

But wanting that and having that were two very different things. Wanting that still tied him in knots.

Having that had proved impossible.

He lifted his hand to her banged-up face, carefully stroking his thumb across a cut on her cheekbone liberally smeared with dried blood. The full reality of what had almost happened tonight slammed into him all over again, and he had to try twice before he could speak. "Time to get yourself looked at. Get these cleaned up and make sure there's nothing more serious that you've hurt."

"I'm fine."

Of course she was, despite what she'd gone through tonight. That was his independent Bree in a nutshell, wasn't it? Except she wasn't his anymore.

He dropped his hand from her cheek. The hollow ache in his chest seemed to physically hurt, his body started to shake again from the inside out, and he knew he had to get out of there before he did something horrifying. Like grab Bree up and plead with her to change her mind, to come back to him again. Beg her to love him again.

The room suddenly felt claustrophobic, and he gulped in a breath, trying to get air. "I need to go to the OR, see what injuries Emma has."

He strode out the door and could feel Bree's eyes on his back. Imagined pain in them, the hurt, maybe, that he wasn't sticking around for her when she'd obviously been through hell and back in the past hours.

His steps slowed and he nearly turned. Until he remembered how vehemently she'd assured him she didn't need a man in her life to take care of her. That she'd never need that, when all he'd wanted had been for them to take care of each other, form a partnership, the way his parents always had. What his father had said he wanted for both of his children—a deep love with one special person, having children together, to form the best kind of foundation for their adult lives.

She'd claimed that his vision for their future had somehow been all about him trying to change her, or be someone different from who she was, and how she'd figured that he just didn't understand. There wasn't one single thing he could think of that he'd want to change about Bree Donovan, except her conviction that children would never fit into her life. He couldn't deny that making a family with her was a vision he'd had a hard time letting go.

Somehow he forced himself to keep walking. But the distance felt as if yet another seismic shift shook his heart, sending the cracks that already crisscrossed throughout splitting wider than the Grand Canyon.

CHAPTER TWO

"Anybody know where Dr. Latham might be?"

Bree had asked that question at least a dozen times in the past half hour as she'd roamed the hospital hallways. The emergency department, the surgical floors, the Trauma ICU, the NICU. She got the same answer as all the previous times, which was no.

Where in the world was he? And why wouldn't he answer his darn phone? She was positive he wouldn't have just gone on home while Emma was in critical condition. Knew that she'd just missed him when she'd finally been able to go see how Emma was doing. Knew he'd been to the NICU to see the baby, too, who was thankfully doing remarkably well, considering his terrifyingly abrupt entry into the world.

But all that had been over an hour after she'd left the ER. Dr. Kurz had insisted on a battery of tests and X-rays to make sure Bree didn't have some kind of underlying injury that might surface later, which had been a frustrating delay. But she'd known it was necessary. Head injuries were no joke, and, since she'd been briefly knocked out, she was glad she didn't seem to have a concussion. So all she had to deal with, which in comparison was nothing, were the aches and pains she felt from head to toe now that the crisis with Emma was over. At least, over for now, but her condition was still far from stable.

Maybe there was someone else who just might need her right then in a way that unconscious Emma didn't. How could Sean not need comfort after the shock and scare of nearly losing his sister? And if he did, no matter what, she wanted to be there for him.

His family was so very different from her own. It almost seemed that being aggravated with one another sometimes was part of their love and closeness, and Bree couldn't figure that out. Her own family's disappointments and frustrations with one another ran deep, keeping them farther apart instead of closer.

She knew from the way Sean talked about his mother and sister that he loved them unconditionally. Knew from the indulgent expression she'd seen on his face most of the time he was looking at them, from the smile in his eyes, even when he was giving them grief about something. Obviously similar to the way Emma had told her their father had loved them. Bree wished that she could have met the important, missing piece to their family. Gone, but still with them in their hearts, in so many ways, every day.

Bree's family? From the time she was little, she'd learned excelling at something was the best way to get her father's attention. Winning a tennis match, or a surf competition, being on the dean's list, getting into medical school. He'd left her and her mother when Bree was ten years old to marry a high-powered lawyer, and after that she rarely saw him. He did keep in touch, though, sending her notes when she did something he approved of, or had her photo in a surf magazine. The occasional phone call from him? Those were surprising and happy moments that showed he was proud of her, and made her feel pretty proud of herself, too.

She remembered chiming in with him many of the times he criticized her mother for focusing all her attention on her only child. Consumed with Bree's life and her accomplishments, hovering and smothering, which drove her crazy. He'd often asked her mom why she never had any interest in actually doing something worthwhile on her own, when she easily could have done with her trust-fund money behind her, and Bree knew her mother's lack of accomplishment and independence was why he'd left. Now that she was older and more mature, Bree felt bad that she'd gone along with her dad's unpleasant comments, though her mother's feelings never seemed hurt by it, thankfully.

She shook her head fiercely. Why was she even thinking about all that now, anyway? She'd learned long ago not to care. Must just be from worrying about Sean and Emma and their mom. Feeling unsettled after such an awful day.

Time to focus on what was important here, which was how Sean must be feeling. She knew holding him, comforting him, would rip open the wound on her heart she was trying hard to heal, but their time together in the ER today had already done that. Maybe he wouldn't open up to her, especially considering their present relationship. Non-relationship. But she had to at least try.

Except it was looking as if she'd never find him. The longer she looked, the bigger the worry in her gut grew.

Until the *aha!* moment came that should have occurred to her when she first started searching. "Of course," she whispered to herself as she pivoted toward the elevator. Part of her dreaded heading where she knew he'd be. Had avoided going there for months because she didn't want to think about the last time she'd been there with him. To feel the deep disappointment drench her with disbelief and pain all over again.

She stepped out onto the hospital's rooftop, and the cool, night breeze of August soothed her sore face. To her left was the brightly lit helipad, but her attention went straight to the benches in shadow to her right. To the balcony railing that, in one direction, overlooked the twinkling lights of the city and the other, the ocean. And just as she'd expected, the unmistakably tall form of Sean Latham stood there leaning against the railing, his broad back to her.

She stood there a moment, letting the feelings wash over her. The good ones along with the really bad ones. Thinking about the joyful times they'd spent up here celebrating a good outcome with a patient they'd worked on together. The times they'd joked and laughed about some silly, unimportant thing going on at the hospital. The times they'd held one another when things hadn't gone so well.

The tender times they'd just needed to get away from the hustle of the hospital and had come up here to smell the ocean breeze, to kiss and talk and connect with one another.

As she stared at his back, the memory of the last time they'd stood here together pinched her heart. She'd been so angry, so hurt, so confused, she'd yanked off the engagement ring he'd given her and thrown it right at him. The blinding, midday sunshine had caught the diamond, sending a prism of sharp white light searing across both of them just before the ring bounced off his muscular chest, pinged along the concrete and dived right off the side of the building.

At that moment, she hadn't cared. Later? She'd felt a deep regret at losing that beautiful ring, and what it had meant. Or what she'd thought it meant. She wouldn't admit it to a living soul, but for days after she'd searched the streets below, finding nothing but bits of asphalt and leaves and trash until she'd finally given up.

Probably, though, it was all symbolic. That ring had disappeared along with the future she'd thought she and Sean would have together.

She willed her feet to move toward him, reminding herself she wasn't here to dredge up and rehash the past. Her goal was to be Sean's friend tonight. To be a sympathetic ear after an unbelievably horrible day and uncertain future for Emma, not to mention the future of the baby who just might still lose his mother.

She moved to within a few inches of Sean's side and gripped the railing, feeling the warmth of his arm near hers. Took in the scene in front of them, thinking about the disconnect of it all. How peaceful and tranquil it seemed compared to the churning going on inside her and doubtless Sean, too. To the life-and-death battles going on that very minute inside the hospital.

He didn't move, didn't speak, and she wondered if maybe he just wanted to be alone. But after looking for him the past hour, she was going to offer comfort if it killed her. Then leave if it wasn't welcome.

"How are you doing?" she asked.

"Fine."

Okay… She drew the cool breeze into her lungs and tried again. "What do you think about Emma's prognosis?"

"Your guess is as good as mine. Liver laceration's been repaired, ruptured spleen removed. C-section's closed. Chest tube's not draining any more blood, so they've removed it. Broken arm's been put back together, and her broken ribs are going to hurt like crazy, but I imagine she'll barely notice, considering everything else."

He didn't have to say the situation could still get worse fast. Why wouldn't he look at her so she could see his expression? His tone was flat and emotionless, giving away nothing. It reminded her too much of the way he'd sounded after she'd told him it was over between them.

"Baby seems healthy, at least," she said, forging on. "Remarkable, really."

"Yeah."

"Did Emma tell you what she'd decided to name him?"

"No."

Not a surprise, really, since Sean had made his dismay over Emma's life choices very clear, and she'd distanced herself from him the past months because of it.

"She'd decided on Wilson—your mother's maiden name. She laughed about it, saying his uncle Sean would think it was a weird first name, but she plans to call him Will. I think Will Latham has a nice sound to it, don't you?"

"Mom will like that."

At least he'd answered in more than a monosyllable,

but he still didn't turn to look at her. Guess there hadn't been much point in her coming after all.

"That moment in the ER when we thought we'd lost Emma. That was…" She stopped, because she couldn't come up with a word even close to how it had felt. She knew how much he loved his sister, and pressed her hand to his warm back as she had earlier, thinking maybe that connection would help him let go and share. "That must have been incredibly hard for you."

"Hard?" He suddenly swung to her, and the surprise of it had her taking a step back. He grasped her arms and pulled her flat against him, practically knocking her breath from her lungs. The dark eyes staring down into hers were again fierce, anguished, his features taut granite. "Damn it, Bree. You were in that car with her. It could have been you, too. You lying there dead on that table. I could have lost all three of you at once, in one second. Might never have seen my nephew, might never have been able to give my sister grief about her choices or her life again. Might never have been able to see your beautiful face and feel so mad at you I could barely keep from going ballistic. So angry that you left me I wanted to punch something."

His voice cracked on some of the words before his arms wrapped tightly around her and his mouth came down hard on hers.

Bree curled her fingers into his scrub shirt and let herself feel every emotion in his kiss. The fear, the anguish. The frustration and anger and pain. Everything she'd felt, too, from the second she'd been able to focus enough to look across her car console. To see the mangled door pressing in on Emma. Everything she'd felt in the emergency room as everyone desperately worked to keep Emma alive. To deliver Will alive.

Everything she'd felt when they'd broken off the relationship that had seemed so foolishly perfect. Today's intense emotions were confusingly tangled up with Sean and their past. From their instantaneous attraction and passion to the final argument six months ago, and that anger and frustration and pain had been nearly as unbearable as today's.

Sean was holding her body so close against his, she wasn't sure where he ended and she began, but his kiss began to change. It felt less about all those consuming emotions, and more about a deep relief mingling with the simple and profound connection they used to have. Softening into a tenderness that flipped Bree's aching heart inside out, reminding her with excruciating clarity how good it had been between them. How delicious and wonderful and like nothing she'd ever experienced before.

"Bree." His mouth barely separated from hers enough to whisper the word. "Bree."

His fingers slipped into her hair, gently holding the back of her head as his lips caressed hers again so sweetly now, so leisurely, it weakened her knees and made her heart thud in slow, heavy strokes as the kiss changed again. Still sweet, still tender, but deeper now, stealing every molecule of breath from her lungs. Shaking, she slid her hands up his chest to cup the sides of his strong neck, to feel the warmth of his skin.

How could she survive without this?

Through her misty, single-minded focus on the feel of him and the taste of him, she became vaguely aware of a rhythmic sound, growing louder. The drone of an engine and the whup-whup of helicopter blades. Somehow, she managed to separate her mouth from his and open her eyes to see Sean's lids lifting at the same time. His eyes were black, glittering like onyx, staring at her. His face was still tight, his jaw clenched. His chest heaved against hers as they stared at one another.

Bree took that moment to memorize his face, and, even as she did, inwardly mocked herself. Memorize it? Who was she kidding? Every curve and angle was forever etched deep in her mind and heart, and the vision of it appeared, unwelcome, all too often as it was.

Still, they just stood there, and she couldn't make herself pull away, even though her preservation instincts told her she should. Reopen the wound on her heart? Their kiss and current closeness had made doubly sure of that, with some serious bleeding sure to follow.

The roar of the chopper landing on the helipad, the wind whipping her hair into her eyes and across both their faces, finally forced them to slowly separate. Sean briefly shut his eyes, and his chest lifted in another deep breath before he looked at her again, wordlessly grasping her elbow to lead her across the asphalt to the elevator.

Bree wanted to bang her head against the metal doors. She supposed a kiss between them should have been expected after all the big emotions of the day. But, oh, how she wished they hadn't, because she didn't need another ache inside her body to join the outer ones hurting plenty at that moment.

Sean stood in silence as he punched the button to the

NICU floor and they didn't speak as it lowered there. And what was there to say, after all, that hadn't already been expressed one way or another? With that "another" way having left her legs still stupidly wobbling.

She followed him down the corridor, her attention instantly caught by how sexily disheveled his thick, dark hair was. Noting the width of his shoulders tugging at his shirt, how incredibly good the man looked in scrubs. The acrid hurt that he was no longer hers— had never really been hers—threatened to creep its way inside her internal organs all over again, and that really ticked her off.

Get over it. It wasn't meant to be.

Resolutely, she turned her focus to the baby as they approached his incubator. A feeling of utter exhaustion began to seep through her, leaving every muscle a little limp. Between the accident itself, the crises of Emma and the baby in the ER, and the mixed emotions of being with Sean, she was physically and emotionally spent. Her next shift started in a mere six hours, and, if she was going to be functional enough to work, she had to get some sleep.

With any luck, it would be the deep kind of sleep little Will seemed to be enjoying. So still, he appeared to not even be breathing, but the steady beep of the monitors reassuringly showed he was fine. Which meant she had to spend only a few more minutes with Sean, and then she could say goodbye. If all went well, Emma would improve and be out of Intensive Care fairly soon, and Bree's interactions with Sean would be brief and limited. Then, in eight days, off to Honolulu for her surf competition, new job and career advancement, and no more thinking about the man ever again.

And wouldn't that be wonderful? Darned unlikely, too, since she hadn't been able to accomplish that the past six months, and even more now that he was standing close by her side, hands in his pockets, looking down at little Will in the NICU bassinet. All too aware of the way his body radiated more warmth than the heat lamp glowing over the baby. Aware of the lines of his handsome profile, of the way his big body made her feel small, which didn't happen often to a five-foot-nine woman.

She took a side step away from all that so she could breathe and focus. "He looks good," she said, hoping he knew she was talking about the baby, and not talking to herself about Dr. Sean Latham. "They don't even have him on oxygen anymore."

"Yeah. He looks a lot better than he did when you first brought him into the world."

"Does your mom know?"

"Haven't been able to reach her. I contacted the cruise line to give her a message to call me, but I'm not sure how they'll get her home. Might have to wait until the ship docks in a few days." He turned to her, pinning her with those dark eyes of his. "Tell me about the accident."

The accident. Last thing she wanted to talk about was that nightmare. But as her gaze met his somber one, she figured he deserved to know at least a few details about how his sister got hurt.

"I'd picked her up from the airport. Maybe you knew

she was staying with me until your mother gets back from her cruise?"

"I didn't know." And it was clear he was pretty annoyed by that. "But go on."

"Traffic was heavy. We were driving through an intersection when...when a truck going fast ran the light and crashed into her side of the car." She closed her eyes and couldn't go on. How long would the horror of seeing Emma so still in that wreckage stick in Bree's brain?

Arms wrapped around her, folding her close against a wide chest. The feel of his hand slowly stroking up and down her back was ridiculously comforting. Comfort that had nothing to do with the two of them and their past and their earlier kiss. Comfort that was partly relief that he didn't blame her the way she'd worried he might. That she didn't have to blame herself.

"You don't have to talk about it anymore. I already got the written report. Just wanted to hear your version. Which I knew wouldn't include how you'd been pinned, too, after the impact pushed your car into one waiting at the light. How you kept insisting you were fine, telling the EMTs to take care of Emma. How they had to open the car up like it was a can of beans to get you out, and that you're more than lucky you got away with only cuts and bruises."

"I know. I just wish Emma had been so lucky." Her voice cracked, and, even though she was trying to be tough and not embarrassingly emotional, she couldn't seem to keep her head from dropping to his chest like a wilted flower that just didn't have the strength to stay upright anymore.

His cheek rested against her hair and forehead, and Bree could have stood in the comforting cocoon of his arms, shutting out every concern in the world, forever. She wrapped her own arms tightly around his strong body and clung. The longer the moment lasted, the more she wanted to stay there, warm and safe. Then she managed to remind herself that warm and safe and forever weren't an option, that she had to work soon, and her body needed rest more than her heart needed Sean.

Maybe if she said it often enough, her foolish heart would finally believe it.

"I'm heading home to get some sleep," she said, somehow finding the strength to step out of his embrace. "I have to work in just a few hours."

"Are you crazy? You've had a horrible day, you're all banged up, and have to feel awful. Tell Kurz you're taking a few days off."

"I'm trying to get all my hours in now, so I can take off the last couple days to finish packing up before I move."

A shutter came down over his face. "You know best. Take care of yourself." He sent little Will a last, lingering look before turning toward the door without another word, only to be stopped by a nurse.

"Dr. Latham. I'm glad you're here," she said. "The doctor has given the okay to step your nephew down from the NICU to the nursery floor tomorrow, then release him the following day."

"Release him?"

"Yes. He's doing great. No adverse effects from the birth. Perfectly healthy, despite being three weeks early. He's an awesome little guy, and will definitely be ready to go home."

"Home?"

The look on Sean's face would have made Bree laugh if the situation hadn't been such a shock, and a very big problem. It hadn't occurred to her to think about where the baby would go when he was given the green light to be released, even though it should have, and obviously hadn't occurred to Sean, either. Emma would be recovering for a long time, and, even when she was stronger, she wouldn't be able to care for an infant all by herself. Though her mother would be her rock, Bree knew. The woman who had Emma's back and supported her no matter what.

Except her mother was on a ship in the middle of the Pacific Ocean at that moment, and who knew when she'd be able to get back?

"Yes, home." The nurse was looking at Sean as if maybe he was a little dense, but Bree couldn't blame him for his shocked reaction. With the baby healthy, his focus had turned to the seriousness of Emma's condition. "I know his mother's going to be in the hospital quite a while. How about I have the social worker get with you to give you information on day cares that take infants? Though you'll need a nanny or nursemaid for at least a little while first."

"Nanny?" His stunned gaze moved to Bree. "Nursemaid?"

Something about the way he was looking at her set off alarm bells in her brain. "No. Oh, no. I have work to do, I'm moving soon, and I don't know a darn thing about babies."

"Neither do I." He reached to grasp her hand. "Which will make us the perfect team."

She pulled it loose and stepped back. "No, Sean. I can't. And we already found out we're about as far from a perfect team as two people can get."

"Okay, not a perfect team. But you're a woman good at everything, and I need your help with Will."

"Having ovaries doesn't mean I know a thing about babies," she said, trying to lighten the moment while staying firm on the subject. "Between you and a nanny, I know you'll do just fine. I have faith in you, Sean." She leaned up to give him a kiss on the cheek to show him she meant it, and the feel of his warm skin covered with stubble nearly sent her lips sliding a few inches over to his mouth.

She pulled back, lips still tingling, and turned to practically run out the door. Part of her felt bad abandoning him, but her self-preservation was kicking in. She had to stay away from Sean Latham as much as possible until she was on her way to Honolulu, before her heart got banged up all over again.

CHAPTER THREE

BREE TAPED SHUT the last box of books on her floor, then sat back on her haunches, unable to struggle to her feet at that exact moment. Compared to the day of the accident, she felt reasonably rested as far as sleep was concerned. Getting there hadn't been too diffi-cult, since any emergency department doc was used to dealing with erratic hours, and days getting mixed up with nights. But the aches and bruises that seemed to have multiplied over every inch of her body, not to mention the relentless headache that stabbed her tem-ples with any abrupt movement, were making it a little tough to get around.

"Okay, Granny, move." As she pushed to her feet, the doorbell pealed through her apartment. She was ex-pecting the landlord coming with end-of-lease paper-work, and her heart slammed hard into her ribs when she opened the door. No landlord standing there. It was Sean.

Sean, wearing blue jeans and a T-shirt and, aston-ishingly, holding little Will awkwardly cradled in one arm against his broad chest. An infant car seat rested by his feet.

At least, she assumed the baby was Will, though the

little guy was unrecognizable. The tiny knit hat he'd worn at the hospital covered his head down to his eyebrows, and he was swaddled with a blanket up to his lower lip. Then again, there was no denying he was a Latham. The alert brown eyes staring at her from under that hat were already remarkably similar to Sean's, and she knew at that moment the boy was going to be a heartbreaker just like his uncle.

Her hand tightened on the doorknob as she watched Sean slowly slip his sunglasses from his eyes to tuck them inside the collar of his T. Eyes that were looking at her with an expression she couldn't quite figure out.

What was he doing here? Showing off his nephew before she left? Maybe his real goal was to show her how cute babies were, as if she didn't already know. But cuteness didn't have anything to do with not wanting any of her own. Not wanting a child to consume her life, whether Sean believed that wasn't the way it had to be or not.

"Sorry," she said. "This is a no-stork zone."

"I don't see any signs posted."

"Maybe they got blown down in yesterday's windstorm." She folded her arms across her chest to show him he wasn't making himself and the baby comfy. The uncomfortable comfiness—could there be such a thing?—that she and Sean had shared two days ago in the hospital had been more than she could handle already. "What can I do for you?"

Impassive brown eyes met hers for several heartbeats until he finally answered. "Help me take care of His Willieness until Mom gets here."

"I can't." Hadn't she already emphatically told him that at the hospital, and the three times he'd called her after? "I've got work. And, again, I don't know anything about taking care of babies."

"You know as much about babies as I do."

"Which means neither of us is qualified. Hire one of the nannies on the list you got."

"When I finally got hold of her, my mother had a fit when I told her I was going to do that. Couldn't believe I'd trust some stranger with her newborn grandson. She'll be here in a few days, and told me in no uncertain terms he was my responsibility until she could take over."

"So take time off from work until she gets here."

"Please, Bree. Just for a couple days. We can figure out what we have to do with him together, then take shifts when the other's working." The entreaty in his eyes, not to mention a slight terror, started to melt her resolve, and she tried desperately to firm it back up again. "Emma needs you. Will needs you." He reached for her hand, brought it up to press her palm against his chest. "I need you."

He'd spoken the last words in the dangerously soft rumble he used to use when they'd made love, and the sound of it made her quiver, in spite of everything. Like the fact that he'd used that same voice when he'd proposed, and look what a disaster that had turned out to be.

But that was irrelevant history to this current situation. And darn it, how could she say no? It *was* a crisis situation, and she was partly responsible for that.

She stared into his beautiful, worried brown eyes. Feeling backed into a corner and a little apprehensive about taking on Will's care, along with being too close to Sean when her heart was far from healed, weren't good enough reasons to refuse again. She owed it to

Emma to help any way she could, and it would only be for a short time, after all.

Her lips parted to reluctantly agree. Then almost didn't when she saw the slight smile forming on Sean's lips, the gleam in his eyes, before she'd even said a word. A smile and gleam that showed he knew he'd won and was feeling darned smug about it. If he hadn't been holding the baby curled in his arm, she just might have shut the door in his overconfident face. "Fine," she huffed out. "Just for a day or two. So how is this going to work?"

"The baby store helped me with everything he needs, and delivered it this morning. Pack an overnight bag, then come home with me now and we'll figure it out."

"Come home with you?" What in the world? "No. I'll give you my hospital schedule, and watch him here when I'm off."

"Won't work. Do you have any idea how much stuff a baby needs? My house is overrun with it all."

"Sean, listen. Helping is one thing but—"

Will's sudden, insistent crying split the air and interrupted her alarmed protest. They both looked at his reddening face before slowly turning to each other. Sean's expression made her laugh out loud, even though hers probably looked exactly the same. "You're looking at him like he's an angry alien who just materialized in your arm."

"What, and you're not? And tell me how lungs so little can cry that loud?"

"It's all biology and mechanics. He wants something, and his vocal cords are designed to get attention, of course."

"Wants something." Sean's brows knit into a deep

frown. "Which means he's either hungry or needs changing, probably, and I left all his stuff at home."

"You didn't bring any food or diapers with you?"

"No, I didn't, and there's no need to look at me like I'm a dunce, okay? I'm new at this."

She wanted to laugh again, truly enjoying the sight of ultra-confident, always-in-control Sean Latham completely out of his element. Not that she'd do any better when it was her turn. "You should get home, then, so you can—"

Sean's phone rang, and he fished it from his pocket. "Oh, no," he muttered before answering.

It didn't take long for Bree to realize it was a hospital emergency, and Sean was being called in to do surgery. "You didn't tell them you couldn't be on call today while you were figuring everything out with Will?" she asked in disbelief when the call ended.

"The hospital pediatrician told me she was releasing Will and just kind of handed him over. So I took him, then came here and...well, you know." He gave her what he probably thought was an adorable little twisted smile, and at one time she would have thought it was beyond adorable, but not anymore. She was immune to his charms.

Almost immune. Working on becoming fully immune.

"I'm really sorry, but I'll get home as soon as I can." He shoved the still-crying baby at her and she instinctively took him before she'd even realized what she was doing.

"What? Sean, you cannot leave him with me! I don't even know why he's crying, and since you weren't smart enough to have his stuff with you—"

"Sweetheart, you're a superstar at everything you

do." He flashed the dazzling smile that used to stop her heart. "There's not a soul on earth I'd feel better about leaving Will with than you. I'll see you at my house as soon as I can."

"But, Sean..." The words came out in a high-pitched gasp, and her mouth fell open as he threw something next to the infant seat on the porch, jogged to his car and took off. She looked down to see what he'd thrown was a key. A key she knew unlocked his front door, because it was attached to a surfboard key ring she recognized as the one he'd given to her long ago. The key she'd wanted to stuff down his throat six months ago, but instead had politely—and, yes, angrily and painfully—placed in his mailbox.

She stared down into Will's scrunched-up, squalling little face. "Just so you know, I'll be killing your uncle later. But I guess for now you're stuck with me."

His wide, teary eyes stared at her for a moment before the wailing began again, as though he knew exactly how unprepared she was for this task. A sensation close to panic filled her chest, and it was ridiculous enough to make her laugh at herself. She tucked him close, knelt to get the stupid key, then stood and squared her shoulders. Hadn't she always said life should be one big challenge and adventure?

This challenge might weigh only six pounds and be a mere nineteen inches long, but she had a feeling it just might be the most intimidating thing she'd ever had to face.

The sight of Bree's car in his driveway did something strange to Sean's insides. Sent his thoughts to days when she'd surprised him by showing up after work, when seeing it there had brought a smile to his face and a surge of happiness to his heart. Sent the familiar stab of pain and sorrow over her absence the past six months. And all those emotions were tangled up with the stress of Emma's condition. The worry of how he'd manage to take care of his nephew, and how being with Bree now through necessity made him feel all kinds of jumbled, polar-opposite things.

Anxious, appreciative, relieved, angry. Pretty much every emotion in the book, covering their past, her near-death accident, her toughness afterward, and how she was stepping up now to help with Will, which he'd known she would, despite trying to get ready for her move, and her feelings about having her own kids.

And twisted emotions about their present, brief as it would be. Being with her the next couple of days was going to be bittersweet. While he knew it would be difficult and painful, some perverse, masochistic part of him badly wanted just a few more hours with the woman who'd broken his pitiful heart.

The second he pushed open the side door that led to his kitchen, the sound that hit him proved his nephew's lungs were still in tip-top shape. Sean winced and shoved down all the emotions roiling around his chest, feeling bad for poor Bree. But misery loved company, so she'd be glad to see he was home, right? When maybe she wouldn't have been otherwise? Thankfully the patient's surgery he'd had to take care of had gone smoothly, so he was able to get back fairly fast, but he had a bad feeling it might not have seemed so quick to Bree.

"Hey, I'm home," he called. It struck him how many

times he'd said that to her. That from the moment he'd met her, wherever she was, in this house or somewhere else, that was where it felt as if he belonged. He'd believed he'd belong there forever. As he'd slowly gotten used to not having her around, he'd forgotten about it, mostly, until she was here again. Bringing the special energy and light that was Bree Donovan back into his life. But she'd be out of it again in just days or even hours, and he stopped to gather himself for a second. He blew out a long breath, then moved through his back hallway, trying to keep his voice cheerful and upbeat, as though he weren't feeling a chaos of emotion in his chest. Hadn't heard the literal sounds of chaos within the house. "How are things going?"

"Just peachy." Her voice was strained and tense, which wasn't exactly a surprise.

"Were you able to find—"

The sight in his kitchen had him stopping dead. There were diapers strewn on the floor, and a spilled bottle lay on the kitchen counter, its liquid half dried on the granite. The little bouncy seat the store had insisted Will needed was knocked onto its side, but thankfully the boy wasn't inside. Bree's back was to him as she tapped away at a laptop on the counter in front of her with surprising ferocity considering she was using just one hand. At the same time, her whole body was swaying back and forth and bobbing up and down, and her rear end in skimpy orange shorts moving sexily all around was so distracting it briefly short-circuited his brain.

"Uh, is something wrong?"

"Something wrong?" She swung around, her hair

flying into her face, a crying Will clutched close to her breast. "You tell me. I've fed him, changed him, sang to him, put him down, picked him up, but he's still upset. I'm looking online for more ideas on how to help him calm down, but so far no go. Do you think he could be sick?"

To his utter shock, the worried green eyes staring at him filled with tears. He'd never seen the woman anything but confident and completely together. He didn't know what to do, but seeing her upset sent him practically running to her. "Bree, honey." He swept her hair from her face, cupped her cheek in his palm and, without even thinking, pressed his lips to her forehead. The familiar scent of her filled his nose, overwhelming the smell of baby powder and formula, and he couldn't pull away. Had to let his lips linger a moment to feel her skin. To breathe her in before he forced himself to step back and focus. "They just released him with a clean bill of health. I'm sure he's fine. Don't babies cry for no reason sometimes?"

"Maybe. Probably. I've checked him out, of course, but Pediatrics gets called in when we have an infant in the ED. So what do I know?"

"Pretty much everything when it comes to emergency medicine, that's what." He wanted to wrap his arms around her, to hold her close against him, to comfort this side of Bree he'd never seen before, but he knew doing that would just mess him up. Make him want things he couldn't have. And the baby was the whole reason she was feeling this way, right? Since he'd badgered her to help, giving her the break she obviously needed made a lot more sense.

He lifted Will from her arms and headed toward the back door, hoping a little quiet in the room would help her catch her breath, and being away from her would help him catch his. "I'm going to take him outside for a few minutes. Why don't you sit down and take a break?"

The eyes that met his were still wet and troubled, but she nodded as he walked the baby out the door and around the small backyard of his bayside home. To his surprise and relief, Will's little face relaxed and he quit crying to look around, as though wondering what the heck that breeze was against his face and that bright thing in the sky was. "Well, how about that," Sean said, feeling pretty proud of himself. After just a few laps around his short, springy grass, the child had gone fast asleep.

He was a little afraid to take Will back inside for fear he'd wake up and the crying would start all over again and upset Bree, but he couldn't stay out here indefinitely. Especially with a frustrated woman in the house who just might decide to grab the bag she hadn't been too keen on packing to begin with and take off so fast she left skid marks in his driveway.

The way she had after their breakup, when she'd stopped by for a nanosecond to pick up the few items she'd left at his house. That definitely was a day he never wanted to repeat. His chest tightened and his heart stepped up its pace at the thought, which was utterly stupid. As though her walking out the door now would be even close to that feeling six months ago. As if she'd shoved a scalpel through his chest, leaving him to bleed.

Stupid though it might be, he hurried in anyway, and

the relief he felt when he saw her still in the kitchen weakened his knees. "He's asleep," he whispered. "I'm going to put him in the bassinet thing they brought. Be right back."

When he tiptoed back into the kitchen after putting a knocked-out little Will into his bed, Bree was attacking the last of the spilled-bottle smears with fierce sponge wipes. Now that the crisis was over, the sight of her in his home doing everyday things brought all those mixed-up emotions back in full force. Disbelief at her conviction they were incompatible in too many ways. Anger at her overachieving stubbornness. The deep hurt as his hopes and dreams went up in burning flames, all stuffed down by logic and realism that they obviously just hadn't been meant for one another the way he'd been sure they were.

He let his gaze wander from her silkily disheveled hair, around that tempting derriere, and down to the long, gorgeous legs he used to love feeling wrapped around his back. He wanted to keep looking. He wanted to do a lot more than look, which ticked him off. Hadn't he just been remembering all the ways he was still upset with her? All the reasons their relationship had been doomed from the beginning, before they'd realized that truth? How bad it had felt when it was over, and how hard he'd worked to get over her?

Staring at her and wanting to grab her and kiss her at the same time he felt like yelling at her showed him loud and clear how awkward this was going to be. So awkward that the thought of calling that nanny service after all crossed his mind, only to be dismissed when he pictured how upset his mother would be. There wasn't a human on earth with more ways to make someone feel guilty than his mom, and the challenge of handling one tiny baby had to be easier to deal with than that, didn't it? Surely he and Bree could act like adults about being thrown together for just a day or two.

"Seems we might have a solution to crying that's not fixed by food or sleep," he said, proud that he'd kept his tone light and casual. "If he's inside we take him out, and if he's outside we bring him in. Easy-peasy."

Bree swung around the same way she had before, but the green eyes that pinned his this time weren't worried or teary anymore. They were filled with the kind of unflinching determination he'd seen in them many times. Times when she'd faced a big wave, or a skilled tennis opponent, or a difficult case at the hospital. Tough and determined and indomitable. He knew it would be nearly impossible to find someone like her again, and a heavy feeling pulled at his lungs. "Easy for you, apparently. And I'll remember your technique. I'm sorry I didn't handle things very well with him today, but I promise I'll do better until your mother takes over."

"You handled things fine. Alive and well and now sleeping are all that's required."

"Think there's a little more to it than that, but thanks for not telling me I'm completely inept."

"Is that what this is all about?" Ultra Type A Bree demanded perfection of herself at everything she did, so he should have realized that was part of why she'd been so upset. "You've never been inept at anything in your life. Maybe you've forgotten it takes time to learn new things, even if you are Ms. Perfection Bree Donovan."

"I've never pretended to be Ms. Perfection." An insulted scowl replaced her resolute expression.

"Haven't pretended to be, but demanded it of yourself to the point of ridiculous. I never understood why your work and your event wins were just never enough for you. Nobody's perfect, Bree. But if a human could be, you would be." Which was the truth, and just one of the reasons he hadn't yet figured out how to make his life work without her.

"You must think I have your laundry done and a nice hot dinner in the oven, too, then, after caring for Will all afternoon. Your definition of *perfection*, right?" Her voice was suddenly tight and sarcastic, and he hated to hear it.

"Come on, Bree." Was she really going to dredge all that up again? "That was your twisted version of what I said I wanted. Wanting kids doesn't mean I expect my wife to stay home and wait on me. I know your work is important to you. That surfing and competing is important, too. Didn't I show you I believe a couple should be a team in everything? Including child care and house stuff? I don't want to hear again what a—"

Her cool fingers pressed against his lips as she grimaced. "I'm sorry. Really. I don't know where that came from—just bubbled up from being around you again, I guess. It's history, over and done with, and there's no point in talking about it." The smile on her face was forced, but it was better than the disdain that had been there a few seconds ago. "How about we sit down and go over our work schedules for the next couple days and figure out a plan?"

"Good idea." He sucked in a breath. Apparently he

wasn't the only one feeling unwelcome emotions about their past. Too many different kinds, and he focused on tamping them down as he turned to the small desk in his kitchen to grab a piece of paper and pen to give her. "Have a seat at the table and write yours down while I make some coffee."

"All the coffee you drink is going to give you an ulcer one of these days. Though I'm not going to nag you about it, since I bet you need even more than usual with all that's gone on. Of course, I don't have a right to nag you anyway. I mean, I guess I never did, but—" She stopped and shook her head, sucking in a breath that had his attention shifting to the outline of her bra. The contour of her breasts in the thin white T-shirt she wore, and the memories of exactly how she looked under that fabric, had him sucking in a deep breath of his own. "Anyway. How is Emma? I feel bad that I was so worried about Will I forgot to ask."

The rueful apology and slight embarrassment in her eyes had him nearly reaching to cup her cheek in his hand, and he shoved his hands into his scrub pockets. How she managed to infuriate him, turn him on, then soften his heart in a span of sixty seconds, he had no idea, but he had to somehow steel himself against all of it. "She's still critical, but stable. Everyone is cautiously optimistic that she can be taken off the vent soon."

Making the coffee was a welcome distraction. He sent up a prayer about his sister's recovery, and a second one along with it. Asking for his mother to get here soon, before he ended up doing something he'd regret. Like shouting at Bree about her unbelievable attitudes, or kissing her until they were both senseless the way he had on the hospital roof, or both.

"Cream and sugar with a little coffee," he said as he pulled a mug from the cupboard, "though I still don't get the point of drinking it that way."

"It's dessert with a little caffeine. Which is normal, though a guy who's still trying to figure out a way to inject coffee straight into his veins wouldn't understand that."

She glanced up at him with a cute smile, then quickly down as he set her coffee in front of her on the table, making sure it wasn't too close to the shimmer of hair covering half her face as she scribbled on the paper. Out of old habit, he nearly reached to tuck it behind her ear until he saw the stiffness of her shoulders, the wary look in her eyes as she glanced at him again with a deep crease between her brows.

Reminding him again—as if he should need any reminding—that things weren't like they used to be. That they never would be. Which was okay. It was.

And if he said it often enough, maybe he'd eventually believe it.

He sat a safe distance across from her and concentrated on pulling up his schedule on his phone. "You already know I'm on call. Is it possible for you to stay here tonight, in case I have to go in? I know it's a lot to ask of you. But I'm off tomorrow, starting in the morning."

"That'll work out, since I have to leave here at seven a.m."

It struck him that she'd be in bed in his house, without him in it with her, and had a bad feeling that would result in a long, torturous night without enough sleep. He tried to distract himself from picturing her all warm and soft in his guest bed by writing down his work hours, until his nephew's lungs and vocal cords went into action again. He and Bree lifted their heads at the exact same time, and something about the way they both froze at the sound, their eyes widening, seemed to strike them both as funny.

Bree laughed softly and shook her head. "Pretty pathetic that two educated adults are scared of a tiny infant. Babies have been showing up in people's lives for millennia. We can handle this."

"This from the woman who was about at her wit's end not long ago, doing the Watusi in my kitchen to try to quiet him."

"It wasn't the Watusi. It was the hula with maybe a little Macarena thrown in."

How he'd missed those amused, twinkling green eyes. Before he could get lost in them all over again, he shoved his chair back to check on Will and see what he could be upset about now. "I'll be back."

"I'll come with you. I need to learn what to do with him."

"First day of Baby Care 101 for both of us. Problem is, the professor's absent."

Will's tiny arms and legs were jerking around as Sean reached to pick him up. "Did you change his diaper?"

"Yes, but probably an hour ago. I fed him, too, though he spit some up. I don't suppose the baby store, or the nurses in NICU, gave you a baby manual?"

He glanced at her, and swore she looked serious.

"Baby manual? If there is such a thing, I want it. But I have a bad feeling that, right now, we're on our own." Her crestfallen expression made him grin in spite of everything. "I guess we'll try those two things again, then take him outside if they don't work."

"Sounds like as good a plan as any I came up with," she said with that rueful twist of her lips back in place.

"We're both playing this by ear, Ms. Perfection, so stop expecting us to do this right until we learn how."

"Your mom will be back before I'm even close to learning how."

Probably true. And the sooner she got here, the better, with this strange awkwardness between him and Bree, bantering like old times one minute, then stiffening up, reminded of the bad way things had ended and how they didn't much like each other anymore.

Or something like that.

He heaved a sigh, then laid Will on the changing table he'd bought, thankful he'd pretty much quit crying, for the moment at least. Maybe he'd just wanted attention. The baby gazed up at him, and his little round face made Sean smile, in spite of everything.

"Seems a little pointless to put clothes on newborns," Bree said, tipping her head as she studied Will. "I mean, why not just keep them wrapped in a blanket or something? He's kind of a little blob at the moment, with his legs wanting to curl up like he's still inside Emma. Don't you think it's hard to get him dressed? And undressed then dressed again?"

"Yeah. But I can't risk having my mother show up early to a naked baby. I'd never hear the end of it." Bree's laughing eyes met his before he wrestled the knit pants off and over Will's tiny feet, opened the kid's diaper to remove it, then grabbed a new one from the pile on the table. "No BM, but it is wet. Maybe that's what was bothering him."

"I'm impressed," Bree said, and that twist of her lips mingled with a surprising admiration. Surprising because he sure didn't deserve it. "No one would know you were new at this."

"You always said I was a quick learner."

"True. Though learning tennis seems a whole lot easier than this."

"Only when you're a superstar, like you. I had to take those damned private lessons for weeks before I could regularly get the ball back across the net to you."

"You took lessons? Other than from me?" Her wide-eyed stare had him cursing himself for making that little confession. She was so good at everything she did, he hadn't wanted to look inept, even though she'd known he'd been a beginner. The first time she'd offered to teach him, his competitive nature had kicked in—probably his ego, too—and now she knew he wasn't just naturally gifted at whacking a ball across a net.

"Maybe a lesson or two." He turned back to the diapering, frowning a little as he tried to figure out the sticky tabs, because they didn't seem to be working right.

"Um, I take back what I said." She pointed at the stack of diapers. "I think the picture on the diaper is supposed to be in the front, not the back."

He had to laugh. That should have been obvious, but he blamed the distraction of Bree being so close, and that admiring look on her face that had made his chest stupidly puff up a little, though she was sure as heck grinning at him now instead. The admiring look that had made him feel like Superman when they'd been together.

He slid the diaper from under the baby's bottom to try again, leaning over to study the sticky tabs, only to be startled by a stinging spray right into his eye. "Yikes!" he yelped, yanking his head back from the stream of urine now hitting his chest as Bree's laughter filled the room. "Can you please help instead of cracking up at my expense?"

"I'm sorry," she gasped in the middle of another peal of laughter, though at least she grabbed a towel from the rack and began to wipe his face. "But that was about the funniest thing I've seen in a long time. Are we keeping score? Because right now, I think it's Will five, and you and me zero."

"Yeah. And we have to turn that around." He managed to get the diaper closed and secured as Bree moved the towel down to wipe at his shirt. The feel of her massaging his chest, and never mind that her touch was brisk and not at all sensual, made him breathe a little harder. He grabbed the towel from her, deciding he'd better get his shirt changed before the massaging made worse things happen to him than getting short of breath.

He slid his shirt up over his head and, when he pulled it off, saw Bree's eyes focused on his bare chest. Her lips parted slightly, her eyes darkened, and he knew that look well. The look he used to love. The look that said she was thinking about the same thing he'd been thinking about when he'd seen her rear end dancing around in those shorts, and the involuntary stirring his body had felt then was back in spades.

"Watch Will," he said, turning away. "I'll be right back."

He washed his face then took a minute to splash cold water on it for good measure before finding a new shirt to wear. How was he going to handle this? Being anywhere near Bree was messing up the equilibrium he'd fought so hard to get back the past six months, and apparently hers, too. Getting out of the house and somewhere public seemed like a good plan. Someplace other than his house, where every room suddenly brought reminders of making love with her, and laughing with her, and planning a not-happening future with her.

He blew out a breath then walked into the baby's room to see Bree struggling with the child's clothes, his little shirt all twisted sideways.

"You do this," she said. She huffed out a frustrated breath and held out the pants. "There's got to be an easier way."

"You'd think so." He reached for the pants but she didn't let go. Both held on to them for a long moment, and he found his gaze fixated on her mouth. The mouth he didn't realize he'd been starving for until he'd kissed her on the helipad. The way she was looking at him had him wondering if she was thinking about the same thing, which then had him thinking about kissing her again to find out. Which would be real smart, considering she'd dumped him and shredded his heart into little pieces he still hadn't managed to put back together.

He dragged his attention from her mouth to focus on the clothes as he tugged them from her hand. Pulling Will's little foot through the pants at the same time the baby kept pulling his leg up to his chest took serious concentration, which made it a welcome distraction. Finally, he managed to get one tiny, curved leg through, then the other, before glancing at Bree again. "Getting this kid dressed is like putting socks on a clam, you know?"

Soft laughter left those beautiful lips. "Never tried putting socks on a clam, but it sounds accurate."

They smiled at each other before he finally got the ridiculous pants pulled up and straightened the mini shirt. Feeling pretty proud of the achievement, he picked the baby up and held him up to Bree. "It was a struggle, but you've got to admit he looks awful cute now that he's all dressed and manly-looking in pinstripes."

She reached out to stroke the baby's cheek, and the sweet, soft expression on her face shocked him. Stole his breath. "Yeah. He does. *Manly* might be a little bit of an overstatement for a three-day-old, but there's no denying he's one cute kid. No doubt he's going to be as handsome as his uncle when he grows up."

Her gaze moved above Will's head to meet his, and there it was again. Something in her eyes that made his heart beat harder and his insides get all knotted up, and just as he was about to put the baby down and reach for her, and to hell with the consequences, she turned away.

"I'm going to take a short walk. I'll be back in a bit."

Yeah. She was feeling it, too, and getting some fresh air sounded like a very good idea. He was pretty sure sitting alone in the house with Will wouldn't cool the heat that pumped through his veins every time she walked back in the room. But outside? They couldn't get in much trouble on the public bike path that wound around the bay outside his house, with all kinds of people going by, right? "How about we put him in the stroller and go for a walk together?"

"What if going outside makes him start crying again?" she said, that worried pucker diving back between her brows.

"Then we'll come back in. Worked before, didn't it?"

"Sounds good." Her smile showed she was happy with the idea, which managed to help him smile, too. "Where's his stroller?"

"Not sure." He scanned all the stuff the delivery guy had piled into the room. "Maybe still in the box?"

Bree shoved things aside to unearth it. "Here it is." She tugged and tried to wrestle the stroller out of the box, but it seemed glued inside. "How the heck do they have this thing crammed in here?"

He tucked the baby into his arm and held the box down. "You should have been here to help put the crib together. That was a lot of fun."

She gave a breathless laugh, finally hauling it out and plopping it onto the floor. "Oh, I'm real sorry I missed that. So wish I could have been here to help."

"Probably just as well, now that I think about it. We'd have gotten in a fight about how it was supposed to go together, like when we built the bookcase in your apartment."

"And I still think the back of it is upside down, which I'll prove when I move it. If I'm right, I'll send you a picture and gloat." She flashed him a grin before she leaned over to pull the front and back wheels apart to open the stroller. The sight, again, of her rear and those bare legs jutting at him and moving around was now permanently branded into his brain. Which sent his libido soaring all over again and his old anger and hurt punching hard into his gut when he thought of all the fun times they'd shared. And how he could keep feeling both of those things at the same time? Over and over again?

He had no idea. But one thing he did know: it was going to be a long couple of days. With unwelcome heat and a lot of cold showers.

CHAPTER FOUR

"WE'RE STILL TRYING to find a room for you, Mr. Grant, but hopefully one will be available soon," Bree said to the more-than-angry patient who'd been in the ER since she'd first arrived that morning, and it was now going on six p.m. "In a big hospital like this, there's sometimes a juggle between getting patients released and new patients into those rooms. Hang in just a little longer, okay?"

She gave him her friendliest, most reassuring smile, hoping a little niceness on her part would go a long way toward making the nurses' jobs a little easier. Nurses who had put up with plenty of verbal abuse from the man, and who had asked her to calm him down since he'd been demanding to talk to a doctor about it. As though there were something she could do to magically make a bed become available.

And as though he cared much what she had to say anyway. There were always a certain number of male patients who, when they wanted to talk to the doctor, wanted a *male* doctor, and treated her and other female doctors the same way they treated nurses.

With disrespect.

Yes, it stuck in all their craws, made her chest burn and her head feel as if it were about to explode, but it was just the way it was. She'd learned that accepting it was part of the job. Discussing it with older doctors, she knew it had been part of the mentality of patients and even other physicians for years, and, apparently, was a lot better than it used to be. Those who cared about the subject were sure that, as time went on, those attitudes would eventually fade away completely. She had to hope that was true.

Sean was proof that some men had changed their attitudes. He utterly respected her work, which had been part of the reason she'd fallen so hard for him. But respecting her and knowing she could well take care of herself didn't stop him from somehow thinking it was his job to take care of her, too. He'd protested that loving someone meant caring for them, that she was independent to a fault.

She'd learned long ago there was no such thing. If a person didn't focus on achieving personal goals and accomplishments and independence, then what would you be? Not enough, that was what. Sean just didn't understand, and it had been one more thing that had led to the spectacular crash and burn and utter flame-out of their relationship.

Not her problem anymore, she reminded herself fiercely. Sean could go find the right wife for himself, and she'd someday, maybe, with any luck, find the right man for her. After all, her ineptness with little Will had proved two things. That Sean wanted the kind of woman who needed a child to feel complete, and that she wasn't that woman and never could be.

Didn't want to be.

Bree listened briefly to more lambasting from Mr. Grant, again gave him the same answer and smile, then moved on to the nurses' desk to go over some patient charts. "Is neuro on the way to check on the possible stroke in twenty-eight?"

"Yes. And I have transport coming to take your teen broken leg to X-ray, and your elderly patient who fell and hit her head down for her MRI."

"Good." Bree glanced at her watch. Her shift was over in less than an hour, and while, normally, she'd hang around awhile to make sure the transition to the next doc went smoothly, tonight she didn't have that luxury. Sean would have to leave for work pretty much the minute she arrived to take over with Will, so if she was going to see Emma, it had to happen now while she had this brief lull.

"I'm going to the ICU for a short time. Page me if you need me." Between staying at Sean's to watch the baby if he got called in to surgery and her own twelve-hour shift, Bree hadn't seen Emma for twenty-four hours and was anxious to find out how she was doing. It didn't matter that she knew she'd have heard if anything bad had happened. She had to see for herself.

As she made her way through the hospital corridors, a strange anxiety rolled around in Bree's stomach, which she'd never experienced much of in her life. Yes, there'd been anxiety before tests in medical school, and nerves when facing a big wave in a surfing competition, or a tennis opponent in a big college match. But none of that had felt like this.

A little jittery and a lot nervous. Plenty of it was from worry about Emma, she knew. But the rest?

From having to spend time with Sean, and the tumble of mixed emotions it stirred up, welcome and unwelcome at the same time.

Walking along the bike path by the beautiful bay she loved always calmed and relaxed her. Walking with Sean and the baby in the stroller yesterday? That had been beyond peculiar. Calming and nerve-racking. Peaceful and turbulent. In some ways, it had felt just like the many times they'd spent meandering around the bay, and more than once she'd nearly reached to hold his hand. Just in time, she'd remember they weren't lovers, barely friends, even, which had thrown aside any and all tranquillity and left her stomach in knots.

She drew in a long breath. It would be okay. Sean's mother would be there soon, and Bree could step out of the picture, focus on packing for Hawaii and move on with her life. Her relationship with Sean would fade to a distant memory. Until then, she'd take her babysitting shift when he wasn't around, and keep contact between them to a minimum. These uncomfortable jitters would leave and her life would ease into a new normal.

Her stomach tightened as she approached Emma's room, wondering what her condition would be. Even the smallest improvement would be wonderful, and she hoped and prayed Emma would be awake and Bree could ask how she was feeling. Could tell her how her baby boy was doing just fine. And was it selfish of her to hope that even a small conversation might help lighten the heavy guilt and discomfort in her own chest?

But the sight of Emma's bruised and battered body,

with her arm in a cast and her body still hooked up to everything it could possibly be hooked up to, added to that weight instead. Yes, she saw patients looking like this all the time, but a friend? Emma, who as far as she knew had barely been awake enough after her surgeries to spend more than a short time with her newborn baby?

No, she hadn't had to go through any of this before, and prayed she never would again. At least Sean believed there hadn't been anything she could have done differently to avoid the accident. The thought gave her more comfort than it should since she found it impossible not to wonder at least a little.

But it had happened, and it was over. Like her relationship with Sean. She had no choice but to move on from both of those painful realities.

"Hey there." She gently brushed Emma's hair back from her forehead, and stupid tears stung her eyes again when Emma's eyes slowly opened and met hers. Since when had she become such a crybaby? "How you feeling?"

"Like I was hit by a truck." Her words were a little hoarse from the breathing tube she'd had down her throat that first day, but Bree could still make them out. "Oh, wait. I really was."

Emma's lips curved and her brown eyes twinkled, and Bree blinked back another spurt of tears. Tears of relief and admiration. It was just like Emma, free-spirited, indomitable Emma, to be able to joke in spite of all the pain and misery she was having to endure.

"Yeah." Bree slowly lowered herself to perch on the side of the bed, making sure she didn't jar Emma. "But you, Iron Woman, made it through. And so did your little Iron Boy. He's doing great."

"Sean told me. That you're helping, too." Emma's hand, purple and black with bruises, slowly reached to cover Bree's. "Thank you. I know you have packing and other stuff to do, getting ready for your competition and new job. Plus you're not a baby person, and all that with having to see Sean, too...well... I know that's got to be hard."

"He's such a cutie. Will, I mean." Needed to be clear on that, since she was pretty sure she'd said those same words to Emma about her brother at some time in the past. "I'm more than happy to be taking care of him."

"The NICU nurse brought him in a few times while he was still in the hospital. I don't remember it all that well, you know? I'm so anxious to see him again."

"I'll figure out how to get him here for a visit, okay?" Bree patted her hand. "How's the pain? Are you getting enough relief, or should I ask your doctor to adjust the meds?"

"The meds are pretty good, but I'm not going to lie. Everything hurts, especially when I breathe. Ribs are killing me." The brown eyes meeting hers were deeply serious now. "Actually, no. Not killing me. I'm still alive, and so grateful for that. If you hadn't seen that truck barreling toward us and swerved when you did, I'm pretty sure I wouldn't be here at all. Saying thanks for all you did for me after the accident and at the hospital, and now for Will, isn't near enough and I can never repay you for it. But I hope you know how much I appreciate everything."

"No repayments or appreciation necessary, and you

know it." Emma's words loosened the bands of guilt Bree hadn't even realized had wound painfully tight ever since the accident. She wished she could give her friend a hug as overwhelming gratitude filled her own chest that they both were still here, but hugs would have to wait for a while. "I'm finishing my shift, then heading to Sean's to take my babysitting shift. I'll check on you when—"

"Knock-knock."

Heart jolting in her chest, Bree swung around, beyond surprised to hear Sean's voice. Also surprised to see Will tucked into his arm, though she shouldn't have been. It wasn't as though he'd leave the child alone, or get another sitter without telling her.

She let herself take in the sight of him, tall and a little disheveled, still sporting yesterday's five o'clock shadow that had darkened through today. Apparently taking care of Will and shaving couldn't happen at the same time, and she had to smile a little, remembering their struggles.

His lips curved, too, as his eyes met hers, lingered, then moved to his sister as he walked toward the bed. Bree stood to step aside and give him space. Or herself space, if she was honest, because she wanted to reach for him and hold him and kiss the tension from his face. Maybe someone who didn't know him would think his wide smile was carefree and happy, but the strain around his eyes and lips was obvious to Bree.

"How's my favorite sister?" He crouched down, holding Will at bed height. "I brought you a get-well present."

"Oh, Sean." Emma's eyes lit as she lifted her hand to touch Will's tiny socked foot. A foot Bree knew had been none too easy to cover, and she inwardly chuckled at Sean's comparing dressing the boy to putting socks on a clam. "I was so drugged up last time, I hardly remember holding him. He's...he's so beautiful."

"Yeah, he is. Just like his mom."

"Look at his cute little clothes!" Emma's hand gently, tenderly, ran over every inch of her son's small body, lingering on his soft head. "Did you pick them out?"

Sean's gaze slid to Bree's, and the secret grins they shared warmed her chest more than they should have. "Honestly? No. I had a baby store bring a bunch of stuff, including his clothes. Bree loves dressing him, don't you, Bree?"

"Love it. Just like playing with dolls when I was little."

"You're not fooling me," Emma said, grinning, too. "I can tell from both your faces it must not be easy, which means it's going to be even trickier for me, having only one arm for a while. Besides—" she turned her attention to Bree "—you told me the only dolls you played with as a little girl were mermaid dolls, and they were always surfing and rescuing swimmers."

"Did I tell you that?" Bree had to laugh. "I don't remember, but I do remember that my dad didn't want me playing with dolls. Had me in tennis and surf lessons and other sports from the time I was six, with all kinds of academic tutors to help me catch up at school. I worked pretty hard for his approval, but I didn't get it very often. Probably why he left when I was ten. I never measured up to the daughter he wanted me to be."

Sean and Emma both turned shocked eyes to her, then seemed to study her for a long, arrested moment.

She shifted uncomfortably, wondering why in the world that stupid confession and comment about her childhood and her father had fallen out of her mouth. It wasn't as though she thought about it anymore. It was ancient history.

"I can't believe there was a single thing about you that didn't measure up to your dad's expectations. But if it's true?" Sean's eyes got a little hard. "Pardon me for saying it, but your dad's an idiot."

"Yes. An idiot," Emma agreed.

Bree's discomfort eased, and so did the tightness that had formed in her chest at the memories. "Thanks. If I win another competition, I might hear from him, and I'll pass on your opinions then."

Sean's brown gaze stayed mostly on Bree as he tucked his nephew into the crook of Emma's arm so she could hold him close. He stood and took the two steps necessary to reach Bree, then one more that brought him within breathless inches. His finger tucked a strand of her hair behind her ear before his warm palm cupped her cheek.

"You never talked about your dad much, in all the time we were together. Just complained about your mom, sometimes. Why?"

"Because he's not a part of my life, really, other than a text now and then, and the occasional phone call. Hasn't been for years."

"Sure about that? Just because he wasn't around doesn't mean he wasn't still there in a different way."

"I don't know what you mean." Okay, she did, but what was the point of talking about it?

"I'm finally understanding your extreme type A competitiveness."

"My competitiveness doesn't have anything to do with anything, other than I like to win."

"Everybody likes to win. You like to win more than most. Wanting to show your dad he was wrong."

She forced a light laugh. "Did you get an A in Psychology 101? Maybe it's true, but it's part of who I am, with or without him in my life. With or without my mother hanging on to every one of my wins like they were her own."

He slowly nodded, then closed the inches between them to press his lips to her cheek. Let them deliciously linger, and she couldn't help but let her eyes drift closed for just a moment to better soak in how good they felt against her skin. "Always remember—who you are is one amazing woman."

His hands squeezed her shoulders before he went back to sit on the side of Emma's bed, admiring his nephew with her.

She watched as the two of them smiled at one another with the kind of special family connection Bree didn't understand. That they'd always had, even when they were annoyed with each other, which had been a lot the past year or so.

They gazed in wonder at the baby and one another, talked about the little guy and his fussiness and perfection and how much their mother would adore him. How much their dad would have loved him. It struck her that someone who didn't know might have thought it was a beautiful, tender moment between husband and wife.

This was one of the things Sean wanted someday.

Someone he passionately adored, someone he could have a child with, someone to help him complete the perfect family he so desired.

"I…have to get back to work," she said, turning toward the door. "I'll come get Will when I'm done."

She didn't wait for a response, but somehow could feel Sean's gaze on her back. She could guess what he might be thinking as he watched her leave, but wouldn't let herself wonder or care.

As if, with their present situation, that were even close to possible.

CHAPTER FIVE

SEAN FINISHED HIS notes on the patient's chart and glanced at his watch. Without another surgery scheduled, he could head home and relieve Bree of baby duty. Maybe even get a fast run in before she left to clear his head and relieve the tightness of his muscles. Assuming the little guy was asleep and not torturing her.

Though she hadn't seemed too tortured when she'd come back to Emma's room after her shift to pick him up. Had even talked to him in a sweet, cooing voice that had surprised the heck out of Sean, considering she didn't want kids of her own. Then again, he supposed a person could enjoy a baby, then enjoy handing it back to its parents, happy to not have the full-time responsibility.

Which Sean had to admit was a lot harder than he'd ever anticipated it would be. As was having Bree at his house. The scent of her back in his life. The daily sight of her that made his heart twist and his gut ache and made him wish, all over again, for something that couldn't be.

Unless she changed her mind about them wanting different things out of life. He'd be lying to himself if he didn't admit that some stupid, crazy part of him had been struck with the tiny hope that, maybe, being around Will and how incredible the little guy was would do exactly that. Make her see that having a child of her own would be a blessing, not a curse. That her need to be some superstar all the time—a need he understood better now that she'd talked about her father—wouldn't have to be squashed. Sean might not be the best at caring for his nephew, but he was learning. Why couldn't she see that they weren't so different—that they could be a team together while she still did the things important to her?

Fat chance, and stop even thinking about it, fool.

He rubbed his hand over his face, reminding himself the kid conversation had been just the final nail in the coffin. There had been plenty of other things proving they were wrong for one another, and he needed to quit dreaming and wishing it were otherwise.

Sean checked out of the hospital and headed home, and with each mile he grew closer, his anticipation grew as well, at the same time he thrashed himself for feeling that way. Since when had he been a masochistic guy who looked forward to getting all stirred up over a woman he couldn't have? A man who wanted to be reminded of failure and disappointment?

A man who wanted to have to take another stupid cold shower?

"Hey, Bree, I'm back." He tossed his keys on the kitchen counter, then listened to the utter quiet in the house. The way it had been since Bree left him. Sure, she'd had her own apartment and they hadn't spent all their time together, but it wasn't until they'd broken up that being alone in the house had felt lonely. The quiet had been relaxing, not oppressive the way it had been until Will had arrived to liven things up with his crying and neediness and adorableness. Sean toed off his shoes to walk quietly through the house to find them, part of him dreading seeing Bree and feeling the desire for her and ache of loss that came every single time he did. He tried to shove aside all that to feel glad the baby wasn't yelling and worrying her.

Except they didn't seem to be anywhere.

Where were they? Surely Bree would have told him if she'd planned to go somewhere, even for a walk. Or at least texted him if she'd had to leave for some reason. He opened his back door to peer into his small yard, fenced off from the alley behind. "Bree?"

Nada. Maybe she'd taken Will for a walk by the bay. Why he felt a weird niggle of worry, he had no clue, and, just as he was thinking he might as well change his clothes and take that run he'd wanted, he found himself heading out his front gate to the bike path. "Bree?"

He scanned both directions without any sign of her or a stroller, and that stupid niggle had him pulling out his phone to call her. No answer. He was about to get his bike to look for them when his eye was caught by a sheen of golden fire lit by the sun. Nobody but Bree Donovan had hair that incredible color, and he turned to see that she was in the bay, obviously giving instruction to some kids who were standing on big paddleboards, trying to maneuver them, while they fell over into the water in the process.

Then he about fell over, too, when he saw her beautiful body wore a bikini and little Will was strapped onto her torso with some cloth contraption. Her long, drop-dead beautiful legs were knee-deep in the water, and the sexiness of her round, shapely bottom in those orange shorts of hers couldn't come close to how she looked in a swimsuit.

A vision he'd nearly forgotten about, until it stared him in the face again. Except this time, her breasts were covered up by a baby and somehow she'd never looked more beautiful.

His chest tight, he took a moment to let himself absorb the scene. Realizing he could look at her all day and never tire of the view, at the same time knowing he wouldn't get to much longer. Never again, probably, since she would be moving to the middle of the ocean in a matter of days.

Heaviness filled his stupid heart at the thought. As if he hadn't heard through the grapevine weeks ago that she would be gone soon. As if their relationship hadn't ended long ago, anyway. He forced himself to move toward them. Probably, she'd appreciate getting Will off her chest—literally—and Sean could try, somehow, to get back his breath and his equilibrium by taking the child into the house, leaving her to enjoy the water without either of them getting in her way.

"Teaching Will how to paddleboard?" he asked as he stepped across the sand.

She turned her head, her vivid green eyes meeting his. "Hey, you!" The wide white smile she always wore while enjoying a calm, quiet bay or a breaking ocean wave was as dazzling as the water. "Well, I saw these boys having trouble out here and decided to help. But I admit we were wondering how Will would do if we laid him on the board and gave him his first water ride. What do you think?"

He'd always been a sad sucker for that glimmer of humor, her teasing voice. He forced his voice to sound as lighthearted as hers did, which took some doing since his heart was definitely not feeling it. "I think the baby manual says he wouldn't like cold water. And can't swim. Maybe floating in the bathtub is a better idea."

"What do you think, Will?" she asked, and the way she bounced with the boy as she waded onto the shore forced Sean to look away for a second. "Your uncle's not into adventuring with you yet, but he will. Lucky you."

The kid would have been lucky to have her to adventure with, because no one was as much fun as Bree Donovan. When she wasn't annoyed and distant and smashing a man's heart flat. "I can take him now, if you want to stay in the water awhile."

"Okay. The boys are just getting the hang of the paddleboard, so I'd like to help them for a little longer. Then I'll help fix lunch. I don't have to be at work for a while."

She reached for the buckles of the contraption, then paused in midmotion to smile down at Will. Moved her fingertips, instead, to caress his cheek and hair. "Did you like the water, sweetie? The wind on your face?" The cooing tone of her voice had Sean listening in wonder, staring at the tender expression on Bree's face as she tucked her finger into the baby's tiny fist, and for once her little movements as she gently moved around with him didn't affect Sean's libido; they squeezed his heart instead.

"You're working tonight?" His words came out rough, and he cleared his throat. "I thought you didn't go in until morning. You better get some sleep, then."

"Will and I took a couple naps together, so I'm okay." And instantly, he could see them together. Beautiful Bree with little Will tucked next to her warm side. Except she'd probably placed him in his bassinet, which would make more sense. More strokes on the infant's face, more smiles at him, and Sean's heart filled with a cautious jubilance that she was obviously learning to love this child. Which was ridiculous and idiotic—even if she did, it wouldn't change anything between the two of them, and he'd better keep reminding himself of that before he did or said something pointless and embarrassing. "I think he's got what it takes to be an ER doc someday—sleeps like a rock, then he's up and at 'em."

"Sounds like surgeon's hours, too."

"But surgery is so boring, doing the same thing all the time." That teasing twinkle was back in her eyes full force. "Work in the ER is a constant adventure."

Adventure. He'd enjoyed a lot of it with her, hadn't he? Wanted to again. So much, it physically hurt.

He drew in a long breath. "Surgery holds its surprises, too, Dr. Donovan."

"And speaking of surprises, I'm wondering why you're wearing your socks out here. Not your normal beach attire."

He wrested his gaze from Bree and Will to look down at his feet, and sure enough his socks were covered with sand, which would probably be embedded in them forever. "They're paddleboard socks," he lied, not about to tell her he'd been weirdly worried about her and had rushed out without thinking. "Thought I might need to help instruct the boys."

"Uh-huh. In your scrubs."

"Paddleboard scrubs." Bree shook her head, chuckling as she finally went back to fumbling with the straps and buckles of the thing holding that lucky baby close to her body. "Where did you get that, anyway? And how's it work?"

"It was in the pile of stuff the baby store brought. And I'm still not sure how it works." Her face cutely scrunched up as her fingers worked, so far unsuccessfully, to detach it. "Of all the confusing things I've tried to learn the past couple days, putting it on, then getting Will inside, was high on the frustration scale. Maybe I have to live in it now."

He couldn't take any more of the fumbling, and reached to help wrestle the thing apart, only to quickly realize that meant touching her smooth skin and the soft mounds beneath her swimsuit. His breath quickened as their eyes met over Will's head. "Think this thing is really a chastity belt for breasts?" he asked as he pulled Will out of the loosened carrier, hoping a joke would diffuse the heat pumping through his pores and the almost overwhelming need to grab her and kiss her and see where that led.

Bad idea. Very bad.

Her breathy laugh swept across his cheeks. "Maybe."

As she slid the thing off her body, he was hyperaware of every inch of her skin being slowly exposed. Her soft, round breasts. Her smooth, tanned stomach. Every movement of her hair across her shoulders, of her slender, toned limbs, and, as his blood pumped hotter, the sexual thoughts drowning out his earlier reminders of self-preservation were suddenly interrupted when she began to knead her wrist.

"What have you done to your arm?" he asked, but the second the words were out of his mouth, he knew.

The grimace of pain on her face smacked him with a hard, shocking blow. The accident, of course. Why hadn't he been thinking about how much she might be hurting from that? Obviously, because he'd been so focused on his sister and the baby, and, damn it, himself, trying to protect his stupid, still-crushed-up heart. Had put effort into not looking at her too carefully. Done such a good job of shoving down the terrifying realization that Bree could have been injured just as badly as Emma, or even worse, he'd pushed aside all thoughts of how she had to have bumps and bruises of all kinds.

And of course she hadn't said a word about it. That time she'd cut her foot on coral after she'd had a surfing wipeout in Hawaii? He'd only found out how bad it was when he'd caught her slapping new gauze and duct tape on it in the middle of the night in their hotel room.

"Oh, you know, it's just a little sore. Like a few other things."

She'd said it with a rueful grin, but he couldn't smile back. "This...upsets me, Bree." With one palm pressing Will against his shoulder, he took her hand in his, careful not to squeeze, and headed toward the house. He half expected her to protest, to say she was fine or that she wanted to help the boys some more, and the fact that she didn't told him she was hurting more than she'd admit.

Inside the house, he tucked Will into his little seat, then turned to Bree. "Tell me where you're hurting." He took her delicate wrist in his hand, and cursed when he saw the swelling and bruising he should have noticed. Should have asked about. How had he not seen it the first second he'd watched her messing with the baby thing, trying to detach it? Every day they'd been together since the accident?

Obviously, because he was a self-absorbed idiot. An idiot who'd been focusing on other notable parts of her body instead. "What all happened to you in the accident?"

"I'm fine. Just bumps and bruises."

"Don't have to have broken bones for it to hurt." He tipped up her chin and looked beyond the light makeup she wore. Really studied every beautiful curve and angle of her face. Full pink lips that had been the best mouth in the world to kiss. Fine bone structure covered with soft, luminous skin. Green eyes he'd fallen into with weakened knees the very first time he'd looked into them.

The face he'd thought for a briefly happy time that he'd get to look at all day, every day, and that he still saw too often in his dreams.

One of those beautiful eyes was going dark and puffy, and his gut clenched at the sight. "You've got a black eye brewing. And probably a lot of other bruises you haven't bothered to tell me about. I can't believe I haven't asked you about this before."

"There have been more important things to worry about."

"Yeah, well, those concerns are currently status quo, so your injuries have been bumped to the top of the list." He grasped her shoulders and gently pushed her down to sit on his sofa. "Sit tight for a sec."

He jogged into his bathroom and dug through the jumble of toiletries and first-aid stuff he should organize one of these days, finally finding the little glass vial she'd left there last year. His sister believed in herbal remedies for all kinds of things, and had given Bree the stuff after she'd gotten banged up in a surf competition. Along with all kinds of other oils, and thinking about what he and Bree had done with them made him breathe faster again.

And what did it say about him that, even knowing she was in pain, he couldn't get sexual thoughts out of his head? Couldn't stop thinking about all the things they'd done together on this sofa? Working to get rid of them, he knelt in front of her. When she saw the vial, Bree raised her eyebrows as one corner of her mouth quirked up.

"You always said that stuff was snake oil, completely unscientifically proven to do a darn thing."

"And still think so. But since I don't have anything that'll work on bruising, you're hurting, and you and Emma believe in it, it's worth a try."

"I'm not sure about any of it, to be honest, but you know how militant Emma is. Says helichrysum has been used for thousands of years for all kinds of things. Who are you to be a naysayer?"

"I'm a naysayer willing to give it a try, though, right?"

For her, and for himself, because seeing her beaten up like this was unbearable. With a little of the essential oil on his fingertip, he carefully stroked it across the offending swelling and purple shadow smudged beneath her eye. Traced the curve of her orbit up to her eyebrow, not expecting the stuff to work, but sure wishing it would, because the sight of the bruise made him hurt inside as much as she was hurting outside.

He put a few more drops in his hand and slowly massaged it around her wrist, into her palm and between her fingers. The sensual slide of her hand in his felt so good, it was a major effort to remind himself this was about her feeling better and nothing more. Then he asked himself if maybe getting the oil had been an unconscious excuse to touch her. He'd been thinking about that practically nonstop for days. Just as he was trying to get a grip on all that, he noticed her knee and the swollen and bruised flesh just above it.

"You banged up your knee, too. I can't believe you've been working and watching Will and never said a thing about it." Guilt sharply stabbed him again as he gently rubbed oil on her poor knee because he should have known. Should have asked. "What else hurts?"

"I'm not going to say everything, even though it does," she said softly.

The instant vision of smoothing fragrant oil all over her naked body robbed him of breath. He lifted his head, and the eyes that met his seemed to have seen the exact same vision. Remembering well the essential-oil massages they'd shared that hadn't had a thing to do with homeopathic therapy.

He gritted his teeth, fighting down the insistent, hot

desire for her surging through his blood. Not only was Bree in pain, the last thing either of them needed was to fall into bed, bringing reminders of all they'd had together before it ended. Ripping up old wounds that had barely started to heal as it was. Brief sexual pleasure, which at that moment he wanted with her more than he could remember wanting anything in his life, would be pointless and beyond a bad idea. She would be moving soon, and he still hadn't figured out how he was going to get on with his life without her.

He managed to tear his gaze from hers to look down at her bruised knee again. Beautiful, shapely legs that were naked all the way up to her bikini, which covered way too little of her. He firmly, desperately, yanked on his doctor hat, figuratively speaking, and concentrated on rubbing the oil around the discoloration of her leg. *She's a patient. Just a patient.* And good luck with convincing himself of that, because he'd sure never massaged a patient with heady scented oil.

"Your ankle looks swollen, too. It hurt?" He knew his voice was strained, but how was he supposed to sound with the feel of her flesh under his hands, and the scent of oil they'd smeared all over one another before, bringing memories of making love with her?

"Didn't I say everything hurts?"

The breathy, sexy way she said that tortured him even more, and he had a feeling she'd done it on purpose. Now every inch of *his* body hurt, too, and he knew if he kept his hands on her gorgeous leg, they'd end up sliding right inside that teeny bikini of hers. To keep that from happening, he summoned every reserve of strength he had and took her hand, putting a few drops of the oil in her palm. "How about you use it wherever you're bruised."

She lifted her hands to her neck, and as he tracked her movements, his attention got briefly stuck on her breasts again. Until he saw her grimace as she rubbed some of the oil on the sides of her neck and around to the back. "Neck's really stiff. Next time I have a patient complaining of whiplash, I'll be more sympathetic."

"It's too hard for you to reach back there. Let me." His hands were stronger than hers, and how much trouble could he get into touching her neck? Trying hard to keep his eyes above her tempting, barely covered breasts, he reached up to gently push her hands away, replacing them with his own. His fingers slipped over her shoulders to relax the obvious tightness of her trapezius muscles. The resulting look of ecstasy on her face, the long moan of pleasure, pretty much unraveled what little control he had. "Didn't know touching your neck would be even worse torture than your legs," he said, barely able to growl out the words. "Then again, I didn't know you'd look like you're about to have an orgasm."

"And I didn't know my neck was an erogenous zone."

With just inches between them now, her eyes met his. There was amusement in their mossy green depths, along with the same sizzling desire he felt pumping through every pore. His shaky control finally snapped, and he gave in to the all-consuming, raging weakness for her. The weakness he'd always had for her. The weakness he'd felt for her from the first second they met.

His hands positioned her face to the perfect angle. Then his mouth was on hers. Moving across the softness of her lips, tasting their sweetness. He could feel her pulse beneath her ear drumming against his fingers, beating as hard as his, and gave himself up to the sensory overload of the scent of the oil and the taste and feel of Bree Donovan he'd missed more than he'd admitted even to himself.

He might have been able to make himself pull back after letting himself kiss her just this once. But her gasp of pleasure, the way she wrapped her arms around his neck and stepped up the heat, her mouth devouring his, had him groaning as he pulled her closer with one hand, the other moving to the curve of her breast. Dipping inside the scrap of fabric covering it to cup it in his palm, loving the feel of the weight of it in his hand, the tautness of her nipple as he gently squeezed, and the way she melted into him weakened him even more.

"Sean."

His name came from her mouth into his on a breathy whisper, her oily hands sliding beneath his shirt in a slippery caress. They moved slowly up his sides to his chest. Every inch of flesh quivered under her touch, wresting another moan from him before he kissed her harder. Deeper. Kissed her until he had nothing on his mind but getting both of them naked and making love with her for the rest of the night. For as long as she was near enough to hold her close.

Until the insistent wail coming from a few feet away sent their lips parting with an audibly wet sound. Which had him opening his eyes to see that Bree was lying underneath him on the sofa, her eyes looking as dazed as he felt, and their chests heaving against one another as if they'd just participated in one of the marathons Bree liked to run sometimes.

If the kid hadn't started crying, he was absolutely certain that hot, naked sex would have been moments away. And did that make Will a savior, or a curse?

Somehow, he pushed himself off Bree, wiping his oily hands down his scrub pants as she adjusted her bikini top and avoided eye contact with him.

"He's probably ready to eat," Bree said, acting for all the world as if they'd just been in the middle of some normal conversation, and not about to embark on serious foreplay and beyond. "He wouldn't take his bottle earlier."

"Okay." Sucking in a much-needed breath, he pulled Will from his seat and got the bottle ready, wondering what to say or do next, aside from adjusting the current tightness of his pants. In the end, though, he didn't have to decide. Bree had her scrubs on over her swimsuit in a nanosecond, then swung her purse over her shoulder, still barely making eye contact with him.

"Listen, I'm going to head out. Need a few hours' sleep before my shift. I'll... You have my schedule, I think, but your mom's coming in two days, right? That morning? I'll plan on having Will before she gets here."

He watched her run out the door as if the devil were on her heels. And, yeah, he probably was the devil, kissing and touching her when she was bruised up and they should be keeping their distance, but he couldn't feel bad about that. Not when the taste of her was still in his mouth and the feel of her made his chest ache for more of her for as long as she was here, no matter how much it would add to the pain of her leaving him all over again. For good.

CHAPTER SIX

"LIKE I SAID BEFORE, Mom, I don't need any help packing," Bree said, exasperated that her mother had called her at work again to ask the same question. For the fourth time. "Almost everything is boxed up already and I'm busy with other things anyway."

"What kinds of things?"

"Just things." She'd learned long ago not to share much with her mother, because next thing she knew, the woman would have jumped right into the middle of whatever she was doing to "help." Invited or not.

"Why don't you tell me anything, Bree?" Marcia Donovan said in the bewailing voice Bree had worked for years to harden herself to. Still not fully successfully, but, with any luck, someday it would roll right off her back without feeling one second of guilt about her mother's neediness. She knew her mother had no one else, but that didn't make her heavy clinging any easier to take.

"There's nothing to tell. Just various stuff going on." Last thing she wanted to do was let her mom learn about the car accident. First, she'd freak out and be on the next plane, insisting on nursing Bree when she didn't need nursing, then want to run out and buy Bree a new car from the trust fund she'd inherited before her marriage to Bree's dad. Want to do who knew what when it came to Bree's shifts with Will.

In fact, it wouldn't surprise her if her mom wanted to bring the baby to Bree's house and stay there with her, pretending while she could that the child was her own grandchild. Which she knew was never going to be in her future, though she'd never understand why. And one of the "whys" was because Bree refused to become the woman her mother was. A woman so focused on her only child that she had no life of her own.

"I'd still like to come see you before you leave San Diego," her mother continued. "I'll travel with you to your surfing competition in Hawaii, since I'm planning to come see that anyway."

Bree bit off a groan. "Mom, I appreciate you wanting to come. But I won't have time to visit with you, and would rather you come later when it's not so hectic. I'll be in crazy moving-in mode, then participating in the surf competition that's just one day before my first shift."

"What? Well, that's just silly. Tell them you need more time until you start."

"I can't. I'm planning in the not-too-distant future to move into the position of director of the ER, and taking time off before I've even started would hardly be impressive." Since her mother was only interested in two things—her luncheons with friends and Bree's many activities—she knew her mom didn't understand Bree's goals and ambitions. And how that was possible, Bree had no clue, since her mom was well aware that

Bree's father only bothered to call when she'd gotten another medal or pushed herself to do something she hadn't done before. That he admired accomplishment, which was doubtless why his new wife was a high-powered lawyer. Wouldn't that have helped her mother understand not everyone was like her? "I'm not about to tell my new employers I can't start on the fifteenth because I'm surfing."

"I miss getting to see you surf, honey. And I can't even remember the last time I got to attend one of your tennis matches!" Bree gritted her teeth against the grating tone in her ear that was full of unhappy disapproval. "Why don't you cut back your hours some? I've offered to give you money so you can work less."

And how ironic was that, since her dad used to offer her money to work and practice more? "I only play tennis for fun now, remember? In any case, I can't talk with you about this right now. I have patients to see."

"Wait! Before you go—if you won't let me help you move out, I'm at least coming to Hawaii to help you move in. Maybe I'll even stay there for a little while after you surf."

Bree closed her eyes, counted to three and decided to pick her battles. As she always did when it came to her mother, who was pretty much a dog with a bone when it came to her only child. "Fine. Thanks. I'm sure you'll be a great help."

"Okay, good."

Her mother's voice was elated now, and Bree felt a pang of guilt at all the ways she avoided being with her mom. Much the way her father avoided being with Bree, but that didn't bother her anymore. "I'll send the hotel info to you about where I'm staying in Hawaii as I get my stuff moved. Got to go, but I'll see you there."

Beyond glad to have that conversation over with, Bree stopped to check the notes on a new patient who'd just arrived by emergency squad. Female surfer, age thirty-four, had passed out after leaving the water. Someone let the lifeguards know, who called the squad. She saw the nurse leaving the patient's room and went to talk with her. "I'm about to check on Bay Three. What's going on?"

"Evaluating for syncope. I think she just got a little vagal, which is why her blood pressure's low. Told me she hadn't eaten much today, just had a sports drink instead of lunch because she only had an hour at the beach. I started some IV fluids."

"What's her blood pressure and heart rate?"

The nurse glanced down. "Ninety over sixty. Pulse one forty."

Bree frowned. "Thanks."

She stepped into the room and saw an obviously fit woman sitting up in the bed, looking pretty normal. "Hello, are you Natalie Groomes? I'm Dr. Donovan. Can you tell me what happened?"

"I was surfing and I think I just hadn't had enough to drink or eat today. After an aerial, I felt light-headed. Came back to shore and I guess I fainted for just a minute." She made a face. "I wish they hadn't called the lifeguard over. I'm sure I'm fine."

Bree had to wonder if the woman was simply repeating what had been the EMT and nurse's conclusion, or if that really was all there was to it. She checked her vital signs again. "Your heart rate is still pretty high,

and blood pressure quite low. Let's start at the beginning. How long were you in the water?"

"It was just my second drop." She cocked her head.
"You're Bree Donovan, aren't you?"

"Yes."

"Wow, I watched you win the US Open at Hunting-
ton Beach last year. Also watched on TV when you
were in one of the ISA competitions a couple years
back—your backdoor maneuver was amazing! I'm so
happy to meet you."

"Happy to meet you, too. Only other surfers really
understand the sport." She smiled, surprised as always
when someone recognized her. Though she probably
shouldn't be, since there were a lot of surfing enthusi-
asts in San Diego. Wasn't that why she'd moved here
to begin with? Then met Sean, which had made it seem
like fate, and she winced at her former rainbow-sky
belief that had turned into such a storm cloud. "So,
you rode the wave to shore then started feeling faint
when you stood up?"

"Well, actually, I had a mullering after my aerial."
A little frown dipped between her eyes as she seemed
to think harder about it. "I fell, and the board hit me
pretty hard. Hurts, to tell the truth."

"Where?"

"About…here."

Natalie gestured to her side and Bree began a physical
exam. The moment she pressed the upper part of Natalie's left side to check for belly tenderness, the woman
cried out. "Ow! That really hurts!"

"How bad, on a scale of one to ten?"

"It…it only was maybe a two when I first got here,

but it's getting bad now. Really bad, at about a six, I think," Natalie said, clutching at her side.

Obviously, this was no simple syncope. "I'm sorry to say, this doesn't look like you were just light-headed. I bet you've injured your spleen, which often doesn't hurt a lot right away. But when the capsule around the spleen fractures, it starts to bleed, and the longer it bleeds, the more it hurts."

Natalie was staring at her with wide eyes. "You think I've hurt my spleen?"

"Honestly? I'm sure of it." And she was. She'd seen enough of that in this ER, and in quite a few surf competitions, to recognize it pretty fast. "We'll get a quick CT scan to confirm. Then you'll need to get into surgery right away."

"Surgery? I need to call my husband! I had today off work, so it's my turn to pick up the kids from school. He'll have to get them. And I need to tell the office I can't be there tomorrow. Or even for a few days, right? We have a big presentation to give, and—"

Bree could tell Natalie was about to go into a serious panic spiral, and rested her hand on the woman's arm to calm her. "You have a phone? Give him a call, then give us his number and the school's number, too, in case we would need it. We'll also let your husband know what the scan says. Okay?"

Natalie leaned back, looking a little less freaked out. Grimacing, she tried to lean forward to grab her purse from the foot of the bed, and Bree quickly handed it to her. "Okay. Thank you."

"Try not to worry. Surgery sounds scary, I know, but we have great surgeons here." Sean being one of the best, but he had Will today. "Make your calls, and I'll be right back."

Bree went back to record her notes and talk to the nurse. "Natalie Groomes in Bay Three has a ruptured spleen. Draw her blood, schedule a scan ASAP, and contact the surgeon on call. Tell him or her to get ready as soon as possible."

"Got it."

"Also get eighteen-gauge IVs in her arms, COS, and type her for four units of blood. She'll need it during surgery."

Bree finished her notes, then went back to talk with Natalie and see how she was doing. The pain etched on her patient's face was obvious, and she was relieved to see transport arriving to take her for her scan. If it was up to her, she'd bag the scan altogether and send her straight to surgery, but most surgeons wanted to see the test first.

"Not feeling too good, are you?" Bree squeezed her hand, hoping to comfort her. "Did you get hold of your husband?"

"Yes, thankfully. And 'not feeling too good' is an understatement." Natalie gasped and clutched her middle with both hands. "I've had two friends who had ruptured spleens, and neither one of them told me how much it hurts, which I'm really ticked about."

Bree had to grin. "Yeah, surfers like to be tough and stoic and act like they just shake things off, don't they? And you're being amazing, too. I'll check on you when you're in recovery, okay?"

Natalie just nodded, obviously gritting her teeth as transport wheeled her out. Bree watched her leave, then decided to call surgery directly and get them ready to take her as soon as the scan was done.

"Did you get hold of the surgeon?" she asked the nurse. "Who is it?"

"Dr. Latham took the call, because Dr. Stone is stuck in a complicated surgery."

Bree felt her eyebrows practically hit her hairline. Sean? How was that possible when he was watching Will?

She pulled out her phone and called him. "Sean? It's Bree. I hear you took the call for a Natalie Groomes. It's obviously her spleen, and I want to get her directly into surgery the second the scan is done. You ready?"

"I'm ready. I'll let them know to just send her here and not back to the ER."

"Good. But I have to ask how you're working when you have Will. Planning to strap him to you with the baby carrier before you head to surgery?" she joked.

"What? I thought you had Will!"

She swore her heart actually stopped for a second, then fell right into her stomach. "Sean, I don't—"

"Honey, I'm kidding. I'm sorry. I shouldn't have teased you that way." He must have heard the panic in her voice, because he sounded worried and remorseful. Maybe even knew she'd felt downright woozy with an instant, cold fear. "I have someone watching him. Tell you about it later—I need to get the call in to radiology."

He hung up and she slowly slid her phone into her pocket, still feeling shaky. Obviously, Sean would have left the boy with someone safe. He'd simply done what he had to, finding someone to fill in, which was the way it should be.

So why did it feel like more than that? As if the connection she felt to Will was way stronger than it should be after such a short time?

She shook her head, feeling a little steadier. None of what she was feeling was so strange, right? Of course she felt a connection to the baby—who wouldn't? After all, she'd brought him into the world, so scared that he wouldn't make it. So thrilled for Emma, and for Sean and his family, too, that Will was fine. And of course, feeding him, soothing him and watching him sleep were all part of the fondness she felt for him.

She drew a long breath, then moved on to her next patient, refusing to think about it another minute. But even as she said it, she wondered whom he'd found to watch Will, and sure hoped Sean had shared all they'd learned about the little guy's habits over the past couple of days so he'd be comfortable.

She pulled her phone out to call Sean again.

"Hey, you," he answered.

"Hey. I was just wondering if you told the babysitter how he likes his bottle. Nice and warm, you know? And how if you don't make sure you get a good burp from him, he's sure to get cranky and cry in pain. And how he'd rather be held when he's awake, instead of being stuck in his little seat."

There was a short silence at the end of the line before Sean answered in an odd voice. Rumbly and oh-so-warm, along with some other note she couldn't quite place, all of which seemed to gently settle inside her chest to relieve her worries. "I forgot about the burping. I'll call right now to make sure she knows. Thanks for reminding me. And, Bree?"

"What?"

"He's in good hands, I promise. So don't worry. He'll be happy to see you later, though. I'm sure of it."

The line went dead in her ear and she slowly turned off her phone and slipped it back in her pocket, wondering why she'd been feeling so weird. No doubt the babysitter he'd found had much more experience with all kinds of babies than Bree did. Sean was probably rolling his eyes at how silly it had been for her to call him about Will's habits. Standing there staring unseeing at the wall, it struck her that, for the first time in her life, she understood at least a tiny bit why her mother still worried about what Bree ate and where she lived and traveled and what she was doing with her life.

Because her mom had been there from the beginning, taking care of her the way she and Sean were caring for Will. And that very second, she vowed to be nice to her mom when she showed up in Hawaii to help, because Bree not needing help wasn't really the issue, was it? It was her mother's need to see how she was and be a part of her life. From now on, when her mother annoyed her, she'd picture little Will and how close to him she'd come to feel after mere days together.

The hours passed and, with her shift over, she decided to check on Natalie Groomes, who was out of recovery and in a room. She peeked inside to see a little girl perched on the side of her bed, and what must be Natalie's husband standing there holding a blond-haired child who looked to be about three in one arm with his hand on the other child's shoulder. Probably to make sure she didn't jump into her mother's lap right after she'd had surgery, which Bree had seen happen a few unfortunate times.

She knocked on the doorjamb. "May I come in?"

"Dr. Donovan!" Natalie looked up and smiled, looking pretty alert, considering she was getting pain medication. "I really appreciate you coming to check on me."

"How are you feeling? Other than like you just had your spleen taken out?" she said, smiling back.

"Not too bad, really. Thank you so much for realizing so fast what the problem was. And here I was sure I just needed a little food."

"Because hitting those early morning waves on days you can is the only thing you think about," the man said, shaking his head with a smile.

"Sometimes true. My bad." Natalie made a face. "This is my husband, Michael, and my girls, Madison and Kaylee. This is Bree Donovan—she's a champion surfer. Remember we watched her on TV?"

"I do remember," Michael said. "Nat couldn't stop talking about your three-sixty. I heard she even badgered some other members on the Save the San Diego Seas board to come watch you a couple months ago."

"You're on the SSDS board of directors? That's such a great group."

"She's on several boards, because she's an ocean nut," her husband said, looking at her with such clear love and admiration in his eyes, it made Bree's heart hurt. Reminding her of the way Sean used to look at her, and how wonderful that had felt. "Even she's going to have to take it easy for a while, though, after this surgery. But we'll take good care of her, right, girls?"

"Right!" both chorused, the older child on the bed leaning up to put her hands on her mother's cheeks and give her such a sweet, gentle kiss, it was like something out of a heartwarming movie.

Bree stared at Natalie. "You're obviously super-woman. How do you manage a full-time job, serving on multiple boards, surfing, and fitting in having two cute girls, too?"

"I just do what I love." She turned to smile at her family. "I love my kids, I love my job, and I love the ocean. Oh, and I love my husband, because I couldn't do it without him." She reached to grasp his hand. "He's my partner, and we make it work, don't we, sweetheart?"

"Right." He tucked the younger child close and leaned over, giving Natalie a kiss even sweeter than her daughter's had been.

The whole scene mesmerized Bree, at the same time the heavy ache of failure hollowed her chest. Bree couldn't be the person Sean wanted her to be. She just couldn't. That had become horribly obvious their final days together, and the dull pain drained deeper into her soul. All she could be was who she was. Who her parents had always expected her to be.

"Well, I'm glad everything went well." She managed a smile. "Best of luck to you."

Barely hearing the thank-yous and goodbyes, she made her way out of the room, not sure where she was going. Until she remembered she was on duty with Will starting now. Except she had no idea where he was.

Last thing she wanted to do at that moment was talk

to Sean, but she had to, and dialed his number. With any luck, he could simply direct her to Will and she wouldn't have to see him until he got off work.

"Hi, it's me. Is Will at your place?"

"No, he's here. I found out there's a day care in the hospital for employees, on the first floor of the orange wing. They don't usually take newborns, but they made an exception under the circumstances."

Her mood lifted slightly since it sounded as if she could get the child without having to see Sean. "That's perfect. Do they know I'm going to pick him up?"

"Your name is on the reams of paperwork I had to fill out and sign, but might be easiest if I meet you down there. If I'm not in the middle of a surgery, that is."

"I'll head there now. You don't need to come. I bet they'll probably just want to look at my ID to make sure I'm not a babynapper."

"Last thing you'd want to steal anyway."

Was he really going to go there again? Because she sure didn't want to, and decided to ignore the comment, instead of getting into another pointless and unpleasant argument. She was feeling raw enough already. "I'll let you know if they let me take him or not."

Bree left the ER to head down the hallway to the elevator, hitting the button to the first floor. She leaned back against the elevator wall and shoved her hands through her hair. Utter exhaustion began to creep through every bruised bone in her body, and dread along with it.

One more night in Sean's house until his mother got there in the morning. Surely they could be civil, even friendly, as they had been on and off the past couple of days. Without any more of the kissing and touching that had made her forget everything but how he'd always made her feel. Pride demanded she not admit that she was bothered in all kinds of ways when she was around him, not the least of which was wanting him so much it hurt worse than her bruises. She could pretend the past was long gone and didn't affect her in any way anymore, right? Be in his house, stay cool and collected, then say goodbye with a cordial smile. She could. She would.

She looked at the signs directing her down the long labyrinth of halls to the day care, actually smiling at the sense of calm she'd managed to find as she'd talked herself through tonight's scenario. Finding the day care turned out to be easy when she rounded a corner. The end of the hall was filled with solid plate-glass windows showing a surprising number of kids running around inside the big, open space full of heavy plastic jungle gyms and slides and toys. But the second she pushed open the day-care door, that calm conviction and confidence was blown apart.

Across the room stood Sean, looking tall and beyond handsome, his wide shoulders tugging at the fabric of his scrub shirt. His muscled arms held Will. Not awkwardly, like the first day he'd taken the baby home. This Sean was relaxed, grinning at Will and the admiring caregivers. One of whom seemed to be admiring Sean more than she was admiring the baby in his arms, standing extremely close to his body, her hand on his back and her hair sweeping across his biceps as he held the baby.

A shocking spurt of hot jealousy jabbed her hard in the solar plexus. And how stupid was that? The man wasn't hers. In fact, she'd been surprised he didn't already have another girlfriend who'd have been thrilled to live in his house to watch Will while he worked.

But she couldn't deny she was beyond glad he didn't. That she didn't have to know it and see it and that when he did have another woman in his life, she'd be long gone.

Because now she knew something she hadn't thought about until Emma had mentioned setting him up with a dating service. Until she'd walked into this room to see the woman practically draped over him. Yes, seeing him with someone else would break her heart all over again.

She gulped in a breath, desperately trying to find the calm confidence she'd felt just seconds before. Just as she was about to make herself move toward the group in front of her, to take Will as quickly as possible and get the heck out of there, Sean's gaze lifted to hers. Something about the way he looked at her left her weak, as if her legs wouldn't work, as if he'd sapped what little energy she had left with just the power of that brown gaze focused solely on her.

Very much like the way Michael had looked at Natalie.

Thank heavens she didn't have to find her leg muscles at that moment, because he left the group hovering around him and walked purposefully toward her, the grin he'd been giving the women having faded to a slight curve of his lips. There was a surprising warmth there, considering his parting jab to her on the phone not ten minutes ago, and something else that made her heart flutter, despite her stern reprimand to that organ as it did.

"Right on time," he murmured, his arms and the bundle inside them brushing hers before he stopped.

"I told you I'd call," she managed.

"I thought you might pay me back for teasing you earlier and making you worry. Hide him under your lab coat, or something, and tell me some other beautiful redhead took him." His voice still had that odd quality to it. The warm rumble that sent her flutters into overdrive. A low tone that didn't quite match his joke.

"Unlike you, I don't have that kind of mean streak." She reached to touch Will's round cheek, because there was no way she could stroke his soft skin without feeling a little more relaxed. Not to mention it helped her ignore the appeal of that teasing twinkle in Sean's eyes. Helped her forget the ache in her heart as she'd thought about him just moments ago. "But it's good you're staying on your toes. As they say, payback is hell," she said, hoping her voice sounded light and unaffected by his nearness. By that quality in his voice she'd heard many times before, had loved so much in the past, and never expected to hear again.

"Can't help but wonder what that payback might be. But I'm prepared to pay up, whatever it is."

This flirtation between them felt so delicious, she had to stop herself from answering with a similar suggestive comment. Maybe it had something to do with the kiss they'd shared, and the touching, and…and… she needed to stop thinking about that pronto before she started salivating for more, because it was all too dangerous.

She reached to take Will from Sean's arms, cuddling him close. The way she wanted to hold Sean close. "While I'd like to come up with something evil, you're in luck that I won't be around to do that," she said, managing to push aside sudden, inappropriate and completely unwelcome thoughts of sexual favors she might demand as payback.

"In luck. Yeah." All that twinkling heat left his eyes. His expression cooled and he took a small step back.

The distance was a good thing. It was, and she forged on to widen it even more. "Am I correct that I have him just until you're off at seven? I'm trying to plan my life here."

"Don't worry. I'll be home shortly after seven, unless I have a surgery that runs long. And you'll be happy to know that Mom contacted me this morning to tell me she definitely should be here early tomorrow."

"That's great." More than great. Which made her wonder why she didn't feel elated at that news. Not seeing Sean and Will would get her stupid heart back into a normal working order.

"You good with taking Will? I have surgery scheduled in about fifteen minutes."

She looked down at the baby so she didn't have to look at Sean. Shocked at the regret she felt that the flirting, the warmth, the breathless intimacy of the moment was over. How could she still fall so easily into all that? Still be such a sucker for the man?

She didn't know. But she did know she couldn't let those feelings wiggle any deeper to get a stronghold. Turning her inside out all over again.

CHAPTER SEVEN

SURGERY RAN UNEXPECTEDLY LONG, and Sean hoped Bree understood and wasn't ticked about him not showing up to relieve her until nine p.m. He didn't expect her to be, because she was a reasonable woman who understood how unpredictable any doctor's schedule could be, including her own.

When he walked in to see her sitting in his armchair, Will curled up sound asleep in her lap, he fought the feelings that washed over him again. The touching picture of beautiful Bree, her hand resting on the baby's belly as she read a book. She looked up and sent him a brief, friendly smile, but not a warm one, and his chest ached a little more even as he knew he should welcome some distance between them.

"Long day. Did the surgery turn out okay?"

"Yeah. Just ran into a few issues that dragged it out, but he'll be fine, I think. Sorry I'm so late."

"Not a problem."

She'd returned her eyes to her book as she spoke. He knew he should be glad that the Bree inside his house tonight was the cool woman he'd talked with earlier. Not the sexy, teasing Bree that kept unexpectedly appearing, reminding him of the woman he'd been so crazy in love with. Not the angry-at-him Bree who conjured up bad memories of their breakup.

But he found that the masochistic part of him he hadn't known existed until recently had wanted either one of those Brees, or both, far more than the distant one who seemed intent on acting as if they barely knew one another.

And, yeah, that was probably smart on her part, but smart didn't feel right. Or good. Trying to pretend their past, their former closeness, their hurt and anger—and, yes, their intense chemistry—hadn't happened between them, that it didn't still exist, was futile. At least, it was for him.

"Have you fed him?" he asked, as much to get her attention, still fixed on the darn book, as he needed to know.

"I was about to, but he went back to sleep." She finally closed the book and set it aside. Lifted Will to hold him close against her, which seemed to partly wake him up as he began to nuzzle his face against her. She looked down and smiled, slowly stroking his face with her knuckle. "Looks like his tummy woke him up again. Do you want to go ahead and feed him? I'm going to head out. By the way, when it got so late, I ordered a pizza for you—I hope that's okay. Figured you'd be hungry when you got home. Should be here any minute."

"Sure. I appreciate it." He shoved his hands into his scrub pockets. All day, he'd been thinking about how he might not have told Bree often enough how much he appreciated her help. Had a feeling he'd let the stress of the situation get in the way of that. Now was as good a time as any, and maybe afterward she'd be a little more friendly. Why that felt so important, he wasn't going to try to analyze, but it had to happen now if she was ready to leave. "Listen. I want you to know how much I appreciate you helping so much with Will. And I know Emma does, too. Even not feeling too great yourself, you've stepped up and been incredibly generous with your time. I'm sorry if I haven't been clear on that."

Seconds ticked by as the green eyes staring into his seemed to suggest she was considering what he'd said. As though she wasn't sure he meant it, and how she could wonder that, he didn't know. He'd never apologized unless he meant it. Truth was, he probably hadn't apologized a lot of times he should have.

The silence dragged on. He was about to open his mouth to say something, anything, to break the tension in the room, when she finally spoke. "You have thanked me, and there's no need to say it again. I know all this has been difficult. With Emma in such serious condition and figuring out how to take care of Will and your mom gone. And…and all this time we've had to spend together. I know it's been hard for me. And I'm sorry, too, if I've managed to make it worse. It's been my privilege to be here for you and Emma and Will."

The strange sensation filling his chest almost felt like months ago when they'd kissed and made up after a fight. "No way have you made it worse. I'm not sure how I'd have survived it without you pitching in."

A real smile touched her lips and eyes, and he had to curl his fingers into his palm to keep from reaching for her to kiss her, as he would have done before. As he'd done when the temptation of her skin all oily and soft had sent common sense out the window. Which reminded him of her bruises, and he stepped closer to look.

"Your eye hasn't gotten much worse." He moved her hair aside, sliding it behind her ear to look at her cheekbone, too, and taking his time doing it because he wanted to keep touching her. "Maybe that oil actually did something good for it."

"Maybe. And here I was hoping to look really black-and-blue so everyone would feel sorry for me. Give me a chance to milk the sympathy as long as possible."

"As if. I know you too well. You covered it with makeup to avoid that."

"Maybe." The curve of her lips had him nearly leaning down to kiss her after all, and it was a good thing Will began to wriggle against her breasts and complain or he might have.

Getting the baby fed was a good plan to distract him from her skin and body and lips and all the things he wanted to do with them, and he looked away from her beautiful eyes to take the child. Then was genuinely distracted when he saw what the kid was wearing.

"What is this...this sack thing?"

He heard her soft chuckle and turned, and the mirth in her eyes had him feeling better than he had in hours. "It is a sack. Since we both are pathetic getting clothes on and off him, I asked one of the nurses how she did it, and she told me about them. It has a drawstring at the bottom. No messing around with pants and socks."

"That's genius! Why didn't the store send some of these with all the other stuff?" He held the kid up and examined the thing, and there was no doubt it would be a lot easier to dress him now. Thanks to Bree, but that didn't surprise him. When faced with a problem, she always found a solution.

Except it had been impossible to find one that would fix all the problems between the two of them.

"And guess what else?" She pointed at the book she'd been reading. "The baby manual we've needed! See, it really does exist."

"How about that? You were right." His fingers again itched to bring her close and kiss that smiling mouth, but he managed to reach for the book instead. "I'll look at this after I feed Will. Thanks for getting it. And for the clothes. I'll reimburse you." His voice was rough, he knew. But talking was better for his sanity than kissing her, which at that moment he felt as if he needed more than breathing.

"Don't be silly. I got the stuff because I wanted to." Maybe she could see in his eyes the internal struggle he was having, because seconds after their eyes met she turned away. "I'm going to pack up my things."

He watched her go to the guest room, her silky hair loosening from the untidy knot she'd tamed it into. He got Will's bottle ready and, the whole time he sat feeding the boy, found himself wondering what was taking her so long. Not that he wanted her to rush out the door. His mom coming tomorrow morning meant no more Bree in his house ever again, and even though it was beyond hard being around her again, his bashed-up heart still wanted her there anyway. Pathetic.

Then he knew why she hadn't emerged yet. His ears picked up the distant spray of the shower, and he groaned out loud. This was definitely not good for his mental health or his common sense.

Picturing her naked under that stream of water, sudsy and slippery and gorgeous, was so erotic, so tempting, it was nearly impossible to not just throw all caution and sense out the window and go in there to join her. The torture of it actually had him standing to put a now sated and sleeping Will in his bassinet then going outside to get a grip on himself. To stare at the bay and breathe in the salty air, thinking about all the ways she made him feel. Wired. Alive. Immeasurably sad. Long enough to get his body and mind back to some semblance of normalcy, and hope her shower ended before he went back in the house.

After about ten minutes, his hyperawareness of her wasn't gone, but it was at least under control when he heard the squeak of his screen door open, then close. He turned to see Bree moving toward him, back in sexy shorts instead of her wrinkled scrubs. Even in the low light of dusk, he could see she was flushed and rosy from her shower, her hair still damp, with little wisps drying in loose curls around her face.

"I wanted you to see the other thing I bought today. A baby monitor." She held up a white thing that looked a little like a radio. "You or your mom can be outside, and if he wakes up, you'll hear him."

"That's great." Her reminder that this was probably the last day he'd see her, with the possible exception of being there when she said goodbye to Will and his sister, felt the polar opposite of great. It felt like an emptiness he wasn't sure would ever be filled.

"I wrote down my schedule for the next two days

before I leave, just in case your mom is delayed some-how."

"Good idea. I'll do that, too, so we're on the same page." With at least one thing, anyway, and the thought made his gut twist even more. "Mom seemed sure she'd be here tomorrow. Though it wouldn't be the first time travel connections got messed up."

"Yeah. Hopefully, though, I won't have to come back."

"Hopefully." For her sake, to not disrupt her life any-more, and for his, to not be feeling this complicated push/pull from being around her again. This fire that kept sparking to life inside, smoldering and flaming whenever she was near, completely oblivious to the reality that it was over between them.

The doorbell chimed, and when he came back into the kitchen with the pizza, Bree had her backpack over her shoulder, obviously ready to walk out the door. How could the heavy weight in his chest at that reality feel al-most as bad as the day she'd called it off between them? He had no idea, and a sane man would have thanked her again and said goodbye.

"Aren't you going to stay for some pizza?" Obvi-ously, he was not that sane man, and food was the only thing that came to mind to keep her there a little longer. Just watching her eat would be better than how empty his house would feel when she left, even with little Will staying with him for a while.

"Thanks, but I better go. Um, good luck with every-thing, okay? Can you let me know when you have Will with Emma, so I can see him before I leave?"

"Yeah." He stared into her eyes and managed to

just answer her question, instead of begging her again to stay and eat some pizza with him one last time. "Will do."

The slow nod of her head sent those drying wisps of hair across her face and she shoved them back as she turned to the door. The movement sent her backpack sliding down her arm, to the crook of her elbow. The thing must have weighed a ton because a cry of pain left her lips as she straightened her arm and grabbed her shoulder, letting the bag slip to the floor.

Sean tossed the pizza box onto the counter and picked up the bag before he saw how her face was scrunched up and that her white teeth were pressed hard into her lower lip.

He dropped the bag and moved to put his hand on her biceps. "Your shoulder hurt?"

She nodded but didn't speak, and he cursed under his breath. "Where?"

"It's okay. They took X-rays of everything, remember? It just got twisted and bruised."

"Like I said before, it doesn't have to be broken to hurt. Stop being so stoic and let me see." He carefully shoved the short sleeve of her T-shirt up before she could protest again that it was fine. Then stared at the swelling beneath her tanned skin. Brown and green bruising covered a good six inches of it, and he swore. "Why didn't you let me carry your bag? You need to be resting this."

"I keep forgetting." The rueful half smile she gave him, the way the golden flecks in her green eyes twinkled even as she clutched her shoulder in pain, weakened him. Reminded him of how amazing she was and how she'd once been his, and that, no matter what, the love he still felt for her gripped around his heart like a fist. The squeeze of it made it hard to breathe. Sent his lips to her shoulder, gently kissing the ugly bruise inch by inch, savoring every silken touch of her skin against his mouth.

"I think kissing the boo-boo is even less effective than Emma's oils," Bree whispered. Her face was turned toward the shoulder he was kissing, and he looked up to see the eyes looking at him through half-closed lids still twinkled, but something else was there, too. Something hot and alive, and he reached for the oil still sitting on the counter before he'd thought one second about whether it was a good idea or not.

"Seemed to help your eye. Maybe kissing and oil together will be the magic cure." Their eyes met again, and just like that he gave in to the need he couldn't fight anymore. "We need to finish the experiment my nephew interrupted so rudely the last time. And here's a confession I probably shouldn't give. I've taken a sniff of this oil stuff about five times since, just to think about when I was rubbing it on you that day. Didn't care that it turned me on every single time." He lowered his mouth to her laughing one at the same time he backed her slowly to the sofa. Their lips separated an inch when he sat her down, and the sexy way she licked her lips had him moving in for more, until she pressed her fingertips to his mouth.

"My mouth doesn't have a boo-boo. So you don't need to kiss me there."

"Trust the doctor. I do need to kiss you there, for maximum healing. As well as a few other places." He covered her mouth with his again, then remembered he really did want to put that oil on her bruise. Right before he rubbed it everywhere else on her delectable body. Breaking the kiss, he pulled her shirt off over her head then poured a little of the oil in his palm.

He massaged it into the bruise as gently as possible so as not to hurt her, then moved on to her neck, which had seemed to please her before. That look of ecstasy washed across her face and he stopped just long enough to get a little more oil. She tipped her head to the side as he smoothed it over her neck again, his other hand sliding down into her bra to cup her breast as he had last time.

"I don't think my boob is injured either," she said, straightening her head to give him a teasing grin that morphed into a little gasp as he ran his palm back and forth across her nipple.

"You're supposed to be trusting the doctor, remember? But don't worry. I'm heading to the next place I know you have a bruise."

He drew his hand from her breast, dropping it down to gently rub her knee. Slowly moving on up her thigh, he dipped his fingertips inside her shorts, and her legs parted in invitation.

"Do you have to wear your shorts so tight?" He couldn't quite get where he wanted to be, and had to withdraw to reach for the button and zipper.

"You always liked the way I look in tight shorts."

"True. At the moment, though, I want to see them off of you."

"We shouldn't be doing this," she whispered.

"I know." He popped her button loose and reached for the short zipper.

"But if you insist," she said, tugging her zipper down and open.

He had to chuckle at her instant about-face, which was exactly what he'd mentally done a matter of minutes ago. Then she wrapped her arms around his neck and kissed him. He forgot about being amused as she stepped up the heat, her mouth devouring his. He groaned and pulled her closer with one hand, the other wanting to touch her now, and to hell with getting the shorts off her first. His fingers found her warm leg again, moved up her skin, to finally reach the slick heat he craved.

It felt so good to touch her there. She was so wet, the sweet scent of her mingled with the smell of the oil, and he parted her more, delving deeper. Caressing her soft folds until she was wriggling and pressing against his fingers, kissing him harder, making little mewling sounds into his mouth that had him feeling as if he might just combust with all his clothes on.

He wanted to see her face. Wanted to see the look he'd loved so much when she'd orgasm, and he pulled his mouth from hers to stare into eyes gone the dark green of a bottomless lake.

"Feel good?" he managed to murmur. "I want you to forget about what hurts. Want you to feel so good all that goes away."

"It does feel good. You always make me feel good. I think this kissing and oil therapy is really working."

Her whisper, her smile, and the way she was look-ing at him were all a serious distraction. As if she was about to orgasm after just moments of the kind of inti-macy they'd sometimes enjoyed for hours in the past. Her eyes were half closed. Glazed, and staring at him the way she used to—as if he meant everything to her—and it added another layer of unsteady emotion to the insanely intense pleasure of getting to be with her this way again. Her lips were slightly parted, wet from his kisses, and she spread her legs a little farther apart to give him better access to the heaven between them.

"Sean. Sean." The sound of his name whispered from her lips reminded him how much he'd loved to hear it. How much he'd missed it. He watched her gasp, her eyes closing before she let out a soft cry. He could feel her muscles swell and tighten around his fingers. Watched the ecstasy slide across her face, and it filled him with a deep satisfaction that he'd made her feel good, made her forget her pain, made her come just by kissing her and caressing her. That in this most primal of ways, at least, she was still his Bree, so responsive to his touch, the way he was to hers. He didn't want it to be over. Didn't want it to ever end.

He kissed her again, slipping his wet and oily fingers to her thigh, sliding around inside her shorts to cup her sweet rear in his palm. The fog-filled lust in his brain had him about to pull her shorts off all the way to take it all to the next level, until one of her hands grasped the back of his head to deepen the kiss while the other reached to squeeze the raging erection tenting his scrub pants. "Your turn," she whispered against his lips.

"How about we share this one together?"

"I like that idea." Her mouth devoured his as she slipped her hand inside his scrub pants. It had been so long...too long, and the feel of her fingers squeezing and touching made him groan and pull at the waistband of her shorts before he embarrassed himself.

"Yoo-hoo! I'm here, Sean! I managed to get an earlier flight. Can you help me with—"

Hearing the voice was like a hard yank on his hair, pulling his mouth from Bree's. Dazed, Sean turned to see his mother staggering in with the ridiculously massive suitcase she always hauled on trips, then stopping dead to stare at them from across the room. Which was hardly a surprise, considering he was between his ex-fiancée's legs, her shirt was off, half of her skin was gleaming with a sheen of oil, and his hands were intent on getting her completely naked.

He tumbled from his crouched position onto his rear, trying to come up with a coherent thought. "Uh, hi, Mom." He cleared his throat and got to his feet, keeping his back to her until he could adjust the obviousness of his erection and wipe the oil down his scrubs at the same time Bree hastily pulled her T-shirt back over her head. "Can't believe you're here already. You've had a long trip. Obviously good, though, since you got here early, yes?"

She ignored his comment, instead sending a long, laser look at Bree before asking, "What are you doing here?"

The utter rudeness of his mother's tone brought him fully alert and had him firing right back. "Bree is here because you freaked out at the idea of me hiring a nanny to take care of Will until you got here, and I'm on call and had an emergency surgery. She's generously helping babysit, despite having also been in that car wreck, in pain, and still having worked all day."

His mother's expression softened slightly, though her breathing still seemed fast and agitated. "I'm sorry.

I was just…surprised to see you. Thank you for help-ing, Bree. I'm feeling very stressed, as you can imag-ine."

"I understand." Bree carefully rubbed the oil around on her skin, seeming to carefully study her bruises, and Sean hoped she didn't feel too horribly insulted or embarrassed by his mother. "It's been stressful for all of us."

"Yes. Terrible." His mom ran a hand that looked a little shaky across her forehead. "So where is my grand-son? And what's the latest on your sister? I'm so anx-ious to see both of them."

"Critical but stable. We can go see her whenever you're ready." But that would mean leaving Bree alone with the baby again. Or maybe they could take him along, and he realized all over again that juggling a baby around ev-erything going on wasn't going to be easy. "But first, I'll go get the baby, so you can see him."

"I… Yes, get him, please. I…need to wash my hands first, after traveling and being around all those people. But I have to sit down for…a minute before I do." She stepped to the nearest chair and practically dropped into it. "I'm afraid I might be catching some bug, probably from all the traveling. Do you think I should wear a paper mask while I'm holding him? Do you have any?"

"You feel sick?"

"Yes." She huffed out a few heavy breaths and pressed her hand to her chest. "Nauseated, and a little dizzy. Light-headed."

He frowned. Now that he was thinking less about the bliss she'd interrupted and was able to really pay at-tention, he could see she looked odd. Obviously shaky, and her skin was a little gray. "Take it easy for a while, then, and see if you feel better. It's getting late, anyway. It's not going to matter if you see Emma tonight or tomorrow morning, I promise."

"I'm sorry. I don't know why I feel so strange."

"It's been a long trip, Mom. Who wouldn't be wrung out? Plus you had the shock of hearing about Emma, and the worry of not getting to see her for a few days." He leaned down to kiss her cheek. Her skin was maybe a little clammy, but from the quick touch it didn't feel as though she had a fever. "I'm sure trying to get here as fast as you could from across the Pacific was exhausting, and you're just plain tired."

"Yes. That might be it. Though I still think I may have a bug. In fact… I hate to even ask this, but maybe I need a bowl." Her brown eyes were wide and distressed as she stared up at him. "I feel like I might get sick to my stomach."

"I'll get one." Bree hurried to the kitchen, then came back to place it on his mother's knee, a frown creasing her brows. She took a step back, next to Sean, and he could see Bree was studying her. Even with his mother there, and not feeling well, the scent of that damned oil on her had his own breath going fast, too.

"When did you start feeling this way?" Bree asked in a voice Sean recognized as her professional doctor one.

"Just now, driving from the airport."

Bree squatted next to the chair and lifted his mom's hand, pressing her fingers to her wrist while she looked at her watch. Anyone else might have thought she was expressionless, but he knew better. The underlying tension around Bree's eyes and mouth had him instantly going from slightly concerned to worried. It took will-power to resist the urge to grab his mom's other hand to check her pulse himself, but crowding her might make things worse.

He realized he was holding his breath when intense green eyes looked up to meet his. "Her pulse is fast. One fifty."

Hell. He glanced at Bree and their eyes met, hers tele-graphing that this wasn't any bug. Her eyes held concern, and her lips twisted slightly as she gave him a small nod before turning back to his mother.

"Feeling out of breath, dizzy and queasy, combined with a fast heart rate and clammy skin, all likely mean one thing, Gwen," Bree said to his mother in a sooth-ing but no-nonsense voice. "You're probably having a heart attack."

"Heart attack? Impossible!" His mother sat upright to stare at first Bree, then Sean, clutching both hands to her chest now. "No. I'm fine. Just a bug, I'm sure. I'll be feeling better soon."

"Waiting can turn a mild heart attack into one with serious aftereffects, Gwen." Bree rested her hand on his mom's shoulder. "You'll get artery-opening meds right away at the hospital, which often stop the attack in its tracks. In fact, I'm going to have you take a baby aspirin right now."

"I can't go to the hospital! There's too much to do to have a heart attack!"

"Yeah, there is," Sean said. And wasn't that the truth? When it rained, it sure poured. He looked at his mom, and the feel of Bree's palm on his back, knowing she was there with him if things went further south, calmed the fear rising in his throat. "But I think you always said trouble comes in threes? We're calling 911."

CHAPTER EIGHT

"Sean! I can't believe it! Is she…is she going to be okay?"

The shocked fear on Emma's face, the tears that sprang to her eyes when he told her the bad news, had Sean choosing his next words carefully. His sister had sure had enough upheaval for one week, being so banged up and in pain and not able to spend much time with her awesome little baby. All three of them had, but it was his job to look after his mom and his sister, whether they thought they needed it or not. Shoving down his own worries to appear calm and relaxed wasn't easy, but he had to make it happen for their sakes.

"It appears to have been a mild heart attack." He reached to hold Emma's hand. "Obviously, anything like this is scary, but our cardiology team is amazing. They're going to do angioplasty tomorrow to open up the blockage in her right coronary artery. They'll be putting in a stent to bridge that narrowing. It shouldn't take her a long time to get her strength back from the procedure, so I expect she'll be feeling fairly good again soon."

Bree was stuck right in the middle of all the up-heaval in Sean's family, too, but she didn't need anyone to take care of her. Even when they'd been together, she'd been too stubborn and independent to allow it most of the time. Except for those massages to soothe her bruising, though he was pretty sure she'd only gone along with that because they'd been in close contact together too long to fight touching one another any longer.

He let his eyes close for a second, wanting to savor the memory of how all that had felt. How he wanted more of it. As if all of this weren't hard enough. Now that she wasn't right there with him, and he wasn't touching her and kissing her and looking into her beautiful eyes, he was able to remind himself of all the reasons sex with her would be a really not good idea for both of them.

"So," he said, trying to focus on his sister again, "with any luck she'll be released in just a day or two. But obviously, she'll have to have some time to recover."

"This is so awful. I still can't believe it. So what now? I want to take care of Wilson so bad, but...my stupid arm and stitches!" Emma wiped her hand across her eyes, and he hated to see how the bruises had deepened. As Bree's had, and his gut clenched thinking about what they'd both suffered. But at least his sister wasn't hooked up to as many tubes and wires anymore, just the IV that had turned her hand and arm purple. And thankfully Bree's injuries had been nothing compared to this.

Emma had asked him what was going to happen now. Good question, and one he wasn't sure how to answer.

But he had to somehow reassure Emma that everything would be okay, because the last thing she needed was more worry and stress when her body was trying to heal. "You're going to be surprised how much stronger you'll be feeling once you're in rehab. I've already talked to your doctors and the social worker, and they think you'll be able to leave the hospital later this week and come to my house."

"Your house? I thought you said rehab."

"They think you'll be strong enough that you can work with physical therapists at home. Get nursing care there, too."

"Really?" A wide smile lit her face. "That would be amazing. So I could be with Will all the time."

"Yep. So, see? It's going to be okay. As far as Mom's care is concerned, I'll be able to help, but I'll have to talk to the social workers, set up in-home nursing care and rehab for her for a while probably, too." He squeezed the back of his neck to relax the kinks. Which made him think of massaging Bree's neck, which led his thoughts to… He fiercely shook his head. "I need to talk to Bree. See exactly what her plans are, and if she can help for another day or so, or not. Then get a nanny."

"Will Mom be released to your house? Or hers?"

Another good question. "Honestly? I don't know. Some of it will depend on how she's feeling, and if she's up to being alone or not. I'd vote for her to come to my house for a while, at least. Bree's been staying in my guest room when she's there, so that would have to change if you both come to live with me." His house was going to feel like a hospital wing for a while, but he'd

take that any day over either one of them having to go
to a rehab facility.

"But Bree's leaving soon anyway, right?" Emma said.
"So the guest-bedroom situation doesn't really matter. I
can't remember exactly what day she's moving, do you?"

His chest got that heavy feeling again, which made
no sense since it wasn't exactly news that Bree was moving far away. Pitiful that he hadn't even asked her the
exact date of her move. Should have, obviously. Maybe
he hadn't really wanted to know when he'd never see
her again.

He blew out a breath. Had seeing her sometimes in
the hospital after their breakup counted as really "seeing" her? No. So her moving a thousand miles away
shouldn't make him feel as if his heart were being ripped
out all over again.

But it did.

"No, I don't."

"It's soon, I know." Emma bit her lip and stared at
him. "And I don't want her to feel guilty about that.
It's not her responsibility to take care of Will and me
and fill in longer now that Mom's sick. That surf competition is important to her, and obviously her new job
is, too. Our...our situation's a mess, but we'll make it
work, right?"

"Right." And they would. He'd make sure of it, for
everyone's sake.

"You have a pretty awful look on your face. I'm
sorry if it's been hard being around Bree so much."
Emma squeezed his hand.

"Hasn't been hard." Like climbing Mount Everest

wasn't hard. "I just have things to figure out about you and Mom and Will."

"Sure." His sister gave him the look that told him she knew he was lying. "Did you ever go on any dates from that online dating site?"

"The one you set up for me, including my photo, without telling me? No."

"Yes. That one." He'd had a feeling that would make her grin, in spite of everything, and he was right.

"Just because I met Bree through you doesn't mean you have to worry about me and my love life." His non-existent love life, unless he counted a couple of amazing, oily massages. "I'm a big boy."

"Yeah, except it's not good for a guy like you to go months and months without a single date. Bree might be amazing, but it's time for you to see that she isn't the only mermaid in the ocean."

"Like your love life has been a roaring success?" He raised his eyebrows, knowing she'd get his message loud and clear, since he was pretty sure she hadn't gotten pregnant through immaculate conception.

Her face shuttered, and he wished he'd kept his mouth shut. As if they didn't all have enough things to worry about. "Sorry I said that. You know I wasn't happy you dropped out of that community college again, but I gotta admit Will is one cute little guy."

"Yeah. He is. He's amazing. I just... I love him so much already. It feels horrible that I can't have him with me all the time, you know?" Tears sprang into her eyes. "This is all such an unbelievable mess. I've been counting the days till I was going to get out of here, get physical therapy, then finally move in with Mom and get to take care of him a lot more. What's going to happen now?"

He hated to see the tears sliding down her cheeks. Until the accident, he hadn't seen his sister cry for years except when their father had died, and it felt every bit as bad now as it had when he was eight years old. "Didn't I say to let me worry about it? There are lots of people to help you and Mom get stronger, and to take care of Will. We'll figure it out as we go. Okay?"

"Okay." She dropped his hand and raised her good arm for a hug, which Sean gave her very gingerly so as not to hurt all the things broken or bruised on her poor body. "If you talk to Mom, tell her I love her. Maybe you can bring her to see me before she goes home."

"We'll see how it goes." He didn't want Emma to worry, but, even though angioplasty was commonly done and comparatively easy to recover from, no heart procedure was a walk in the park. "I'm going to check on Mom one more time, then get back to relieve Bree. I think she has to be at work early."

"That's Bree. Superachiever." Emma's lip twisted. "She'd never talked to me about her dad before, and how he only seemed to care about her when she was doing something great. Did she tell you when you were dating? That must be why she competes at everything like the devil's on her tail or something, you know?"

"I know." Too well. Her need to compete and outdo herself was part of the reason they'd had conflicts over how much she traveled. Why she'd ruled out having any kids. And no amount of talking to her about being able to have the best of both worlds had convinced her otherwise.

He leaned down to kiss Emma's cheek. "See you tomorrow, and I'll let you know how Mom's doing then."

Once in his mother's room, he was glad to see she was feeling comfortable and not horribly worried about having the angioplasty procedure tomorrow. "You look good, Mom."

"I know that can't be true," she said. She managed a smile, but her eyelids were drooping. "I feel like I've been dragged backwards through a knothole."

His dad's favorite saying. He grinned at his mom, reaching for her hand. "Tomorrow they'll pull you back the other way, and you'll be feeling fine again."

"Spoken like a surgeon. I bet your definition of *fine* and mine aren't exactly the same."

"Maybe." Yeah, his definition meant "alive and reasonably well," and he prayed everything would go smoothly during the procedure. "Get a good night's sleep, or at least as good as is possible in the hospital. You've got to be exhausted."

"I am tired, but I want to tell you something." She squeezed his hand. "Your dad would be so proud of you. I know he asked you to take care of us, and while I certainly never pictured this kind of thing, you've done more than anyone could expect. Thank you."

"No thanks necessary, Mom. It's my job to take care of you and Emma, not to mention that I love you both. I'm glad we're all together here."

"Me, too. And like your dad, I can't wait for the day you have a wonderful family of your own."

Of his own. Not going to happen for a long time.

He crept out as soon as her eyes were closed to let her sleep. Feeling as okay with her situation as was possible to feel under the circumstances, he headed to his car. Once he was sitting inside it, the tension that had tightened every muscle for the past three hours, for the past three days, unspooled, and the exhaustion that crept through him just might rival what his poor mother was feeling.

He dropped his head back against the seat. Thankfully he'd managed to keep it together after the accident to be there for his sister and care for Will. Endure the torturous pleasure of being around Bree again. And as he sat there staring out across the hospital parking lot, brightly lit by rows of lights illuminating the way, his thoughts became focused on her. Again.

His life sure had been full of a lot of dark these past days. Bree was a big part of that dark, and yet she was the light, too. Helping him find his way through the crises that kept on coming. A light he'd counted on too much when he shouldn't have let that happen. And it was something he couldn't allow himself to do for much longer.

His mother and sister and nephew were his responsibility. Had been since his dad died, and more than anything he wanted to be the kind of man his father had been. A man who worked hard, but put his family first. A man who had adored his wife and raised his kids to be whoever they wanted to be. A man who'd faced life's challenges head-on, including the cancer that eventually took his life.

He was trying to be that kind of man. Which meant relying on Bree was wrong. She had her life and her plans, which no longer included him, and, though that reality still hurt more than he'd ever admit, it was just the way things had to be.

He closed his eyes, and let himself think about how her mouth had tasted, how her skin had felt beneath his hands, how she'd looked when she'd climaxed from his touch. He'd wanted to see that, feel that again, but it wasn't enough. He'd wanted more. She'd wanted more, too, and if his mother hadn't shown up, he knew exactly what would have happened next.

All those thoughts made his body stir and his breath shorten, and he knew he couldn't trust himself to not start things right back up the second he walked in the door, and what would that accomplish? A few hours of great sex like that they used to share, then even more pain than all that he still carried around in his stupid heart over her?

Time for a new plan. He couldn't take advantage of Bree any longer. Tomorrow, he'd make other arrangements for Will and figure out the future. A future without Bree.

Again. And he knew with certainty it was going to feel every bit as unbearable as the first time.

Bree paced Sean's house, first with a fussy Will, then more after he'd gone back to sleep. Sitting to read the baby book, she found she couldn't concentrate. Tried to watch TV, and gave up on that to pace some more. Hours passed, and still no sign of Sean. He'd called from the hospital to say his mother was being admitted to the cardiac care unit. The echocardiogram had shown a stricture, and they were going to perform angioplasty on her tomorrow.

How was Sean going to cope now?

Thank heavens it looked as if Gwen's heart attack had been a comparatively mild one, but still. She'd likely be in the hospital an extra day to recover from the angioplasty procedure before they released her. It wouldn't be the best plan for her to go to her own house right away, unless she had someone to check on her as she recovered. And even if she was feeling all right, there was no way she should have the responsibility to care for Will alone until she was stronger.

If his mother had to come to Sean's house, then what? She'd have to stay in the room Bree was currently sleeping in. Surely after this latest catastrophe, both Gwen and Sean would realize it was time to hire a nanny. And how exactly did a person go about doing that? Getting the right person was important, and she had a feeling that might not be easy. Thinking of an inadequate caregiver for Will made the pit of her stomach feel queasy.

Still, the unexpected and overwhelming intimacy she'd shared with Sean made it obvious she absolutely shouldn't stay in the house alone with Sean while he was home and on call. Their kisses, the touch of his hands, the memories of how good it had been between them for a while, all had made it impossible to resist how wonderful it felt. And resisting wanting to take it further. Sean had obviously had the same problem. And she was certain he felt just as she did—that getting physical right before she moved away would just bring all the buried pain to the surface again.

At that moment, it hadn't mattered. If his mother hadn't come in when she did, there was not one doubt in Bree's mind that common sense would have flown out the window. They would have ended up naked on the floor, mindlessly kissing and making love then probably doing it all over again in the bedroom, like old times.

She'd missed all of that so much. More than she'd even admitted to herself until tonight.

Will squawked, and she got him from his bassinet, pacing the room some more as she absently jiggled him, her mind going right back to the oily delight she and Sean had shared. Except history had proved great sex didn't fix a problem relationship, hadn't it? And what did it say about her that she couldn't get sex with Sean off her mind, when the man had just had one more worry piled onto him? She had to somehow concentrate on how to be here for him as a friend. Just a friend.

In the middle of her scolding lecture to herself, she heard the click of the doorknob. Sean stepped through the doorway from the garage, and her gaze zeroed in on his broad shoulders, his slightly messy hair, the sexy five o'clock shadow on his jaw.

And the beautiful brown eyes that looked beyond tired, the creases at the corners noticeably deeper. His body moving slowly into the room looked fatigued, too, his measured steps so unlike his usual easy gait. Her heart tumbled over and flattened at what this man she would never stop caring about was going through right now.

He stopped a few feet from her, his weary eyes looking at her with an odd expression. "Have to say, you've gotten darned good at taking care of Will. Look beautiful holding a baby. Seems like you've got him sleeping like a rock."

She looked down at the child in her arms, and had to smile at the way his little rosebud lips were parted as he breathed slowly and deeply, his surprisingly dark lashes fanning his round cheeks. "He's so precious. I…I'm going to miss him."

Sean just kept looking at her, his expression somber now.

She moved to put Will in the bassinet they'd decided to set up in the living room, then turned back to Sean. Closed the gap between them and lifted her hand to his stubbly cheek.

"To say you've had a terrible week doesn't quite describe it, does it?"

He put his hand on top of hers. He slowly turned his head to press his lips to her palm.

"No. But here's the thing. There's you, in the middle of it all. You've been part of what's made it terrible." His mouth lingered on her hand, his warm breath a caress. "And you're the only thing that's made it less terrible. Made it possible to handle it all."

Oh, my. His words against her skin sent a shiver down her spine and a warmth to her heart. "I'm glad to have been here to help."

"I don't know what I would have done if you hadn't been here to pick up the slack when I couldn't. Which I probably shouldn't have asked you to do, since you're not exactly in tip-top shape yourself. I'm sorry to have been so dense about that."

"Not dense. Busy. And that's what friends are for," she whispered, her throat closing, because what she felt for him was so much more than friendship. "We're still friends, even if we aren't a couple anymore, right?"

He shook his head slightly, and as he did his lips slipped across her palm before he dropped their hands to his side, fingers entwined. His unguarded gaze lifted to hers. "I can't be just friends with you, Bree. Maybe someday, but not now. Not when I've been wanting you, wanting to hold you and make love with you every minute we've been together the past few days. Not when it still hurts so bad that you left me."

"I didn't leave you. It just…couldn't work out. You know that."

"I know." The eyes staring into hers held stark regret. A deep ache. She recognized it. Felt the same bottomless sorrow in every crevice of her heart, and she knew it wouldn't be whole again, truly happy again, for a painfully long time. "But I've missed you so damned much."

"I've missed you, too." Her bruised heart seemed to lift and lodge in her throat. So true. So much. And if he could admit it, why couldn't she expose her pain to him, too? Her horrible sense of failure?

"You felt more right than anyone ever had," he said. "I'd be lying if I said I don't still want you more than I can handle." He wrapped his arm around her waist. "I promised myself I'd keep my distance from you. Apologize for earlier, and have you head on home. But looking at you now, I can't. I'm too worn down to fight it anymore."

And then he kissed her. Exerting just enough pressure to weaken her knees and send her kissing him back with something that felt a little desperate. Wanting him so much, as she had when he'd kissed and touched her earlier. Wanting to make him feel better. To make herself feel better. To toss aside, for just this moment, all worries and just feel.

His arms brought her closer as their kiss deepened, and she could feel the hard, fast thump of his heart beneath her palms as she pressed them against his chest. She moved her hands down, sliding them up inside his scrub shirt to feel his warm skin, feel the soft hair on his hard stomach and chest. Sent one hand lower to caress his erection, gently squeezing, and loved that he trembled at her touch.

He grasped her hand and brought it back to his stomach, pulling his mouth from hers to track its moist heat up her jaw to her cheek. "I don't have much reserve strength right now, and if you keep touching me like that I can't promise what might happen."

"Fair's fair. You made me come apart a little earlier, if I recall. My turn now."

"No, it's our turn." His gaze hot, he had her T-shirt up and off before she could blink. He dropped his mouth to kiss the curve of her breasts, his hands cupping them through her bra. "I didn't get to give these enough attention earlier. They're every bit as beautiful as I remember." He suddenly lifted his head, his eyes darkened with desire. "I don't remember this bra. Sexy."

"Had to buy a few new ones, since I didn't have you around to make me feel sexy." She regretted that admission the second she said it. Until his talented surgeon hands had the bra flicked off in two seconds, and she instantly forgot about it as he resumed his slow exploration of her breasts with his hands and tongue.

"That makes no sense." His breath brushed warmly against her skin. "Believe me, sweetheart. You're the sexiest woman in the universe no matter what you're wearing."

One hand slipped around to the bare skin on her back to pull her close as he drew one nipple into his mouth. Gently sucked as he rolled the other within his fingers until it peaked and tightened at the same time everything inside her reacted the same way. She held his head in her hands, gasping as he moved to moisten the other nipple, already aching and quivering, making her feel as if she might orgasm just from his mouth and teeth on her breast. "Are you trying to make me come again? Because that would be embarrassing."

"Embarrassing?" He lifted glittering eyes to her as a slow smile curved his lips. "*Gratifying* would be my word. Beyond gratified is exactly how I felt a few hours ago."

"But I want you to feel something else right now." She drew a breath and managed to pull back, away from the sensual feel of what he'd been doing to her. She took his hand and he let her guide him to his bedroom, taking the baby monitor with her. "You realize you're making my knees so weak, I need to sit down or lie down before I fall down. And making love in your big bed sounds a whole lot better than the cold tile floor."

She yanked back the sheets, turned him around next to the bed and pulled his shirt up to expose his taut stomach, thankful he took over and pulled it all the way off much quicker than she would have managed. She slid her thumbs into the waistband of his scrubs, lowering them to the floor. His erection pushed hard against his underwear, and she shoved that down, too, leaving him breathtakingly naked in front of her as she pushed him to sit on the side of the bed.

For a long moment, she just stood there, taking in the view of his beautiful body. The body she'd explored so thoroughly all the times they'd made love, she could be blindfolded and still find every dimple, every small scar, every one of his most sensitive spots. Let herself savor the sight of his sinewy muscles, his tanned skin, the jut of his erection. Revel in the way he was looking at her now. As if she were all that mattered, and the world had shrunk to just the two of them, being together again.

She'd missed this. Missed *him*. Her heart dancing double time, she waited to be singed by regret, by the ache of failure, but it didn't come. All she felt was a deep want for him, to share with him once more the kind of shattering intimacy she'd never felt with another man.

"There's a problem here," he growled. "I'm naked, and you're not."

He reached for her, but she evaded his grasp. "My turn, remember?"

"Even with sex, you can't control having to win."

"I plan on it being a win-win." She shimmied until the sweats she'd put on in the evening chill slid to the floor, revealing the thong she'd stuffed into her backpack with her other clothes. She gave a little kick, but the wide band of the sweatpant leg stayed on her ankle, and she intentionally bent over very slowly to wrest them off her feet one at a time.

"You're trying to torture me." His voice was hoarse,

his gaze hot. "Since when do you wear a thong when you're getting comfortable?"

"It was all I brought. Sorry."

"You're not sorry. I seem to remember that sexually tormenting me was one of your favorite pastimes."

"You want me to apologize for that?"

"Hell, no."

She had to laugh at the expression on his face as she pulled her thong off before closing the gap between them to straddle him. Pressed her body close to his naked torso and kissed him. Stroked his tongue with hers as she reached for him, caressing him everywhere possible, thrilled at the way his erection throbbed beneath her palm. At the groan her kisses and touch pulled from his chest.

Then thrilled even more when his hands slid up over her breasts, down her sides and inside her thighs to touch her the way he had earlier. It all felt so good, her brain got sidetracked and her hands paused in their caresses before she remembered she was seducing him.

He paused momentarily to get a condom from his nightstand. "I need to be inside you. Now."

And with just that much warning, he lifted her as if she weighed nothing, and settled her against him. The feel of his hardness rubbing her moist flesh had her moving against him, wrapping her arms around his neck and pressing her breasts to his chest and kissing him for all she was worth, having completely forgotten anything but how he made her feel.

"Now, Bree. I'm sorry." He lifted her up and slowly brought her down on his erection, filling her until she gasped with the intense pleasure of it. "We'll go slower next time, I promise."

As he moved her up and down in a rhythm that started out slow and steady, the tiniest corner of her mind heard his words. *Next time.* Which caught her heart with a sharp barb.

There wouldn't be a next time.

"We only have tonight," she said, staring into the darkened depths of his eyes.

"I know." He kept the slow pace, drawing out the pleasure, as his mouth met hers again. "Doesn't mean there can't be a next time. And a next. With Will probably interrupting us in the middle somewhere. Right?"

She had to laugh in surprise, breathy though it was. "Right."

"Glad we're in agreement. For once."

His words might have stabbed, but the way he stepped up the pace left no room for regret or anger or sadness. Only sensation as he filled her completely, stealing her breath. As if on their own, her hips caught the devastating rhythm, increased it, until both of them were gasping. Moving with a speed that felt frantic, as though they were chasing something they'd lost. That they knew they'd never find again.

"Bree."

Her name came from his lips on a reverent sigh, and she knew he felt it, too. And as they stared into one another's eyes, her body convulsing with the ecstasy of their physical pleasure, her heart convulsed with something else altogether. An overflowing fullness, pricked by the terrifying conviction that no one would ever do for her heart and body what Sean could do. She knew it with every ounce of her being.

Why, oh, why couldn't their brains have been on the same perfect plane as the rest of them?

CHAPTER NINE

SEAN PROPPED HIMSELF on his elbow and looked at the warm humans lying asleep in his bed. Beautiful Bree, with her satiny skin, her amazing hair tossed around her head like a shining halo of strawberries and gold. The delicate arch of her brows, and lips even sweeter than he'd remembered, which seemed impossible. Waking up to her there, like so many times before, had sent a sweet ache to his heart, and he'd taken as long as possible to slip a strand of silken hair away from her eye, loving how the softness of her hair and skin felt beneath his fingertip.

Wilson was tucked between them, his little face smiling at some baby dream, or maybe it was gas, but either way it made Sean smile, too. The child had woken an hour ago, and Sean had jumped up to get him, wanting Bree to get a solid night's sleep for a change. Luckily she'd stirred only a moment, then gone right back to sleep, much like Will after he'd had his bottle.

Looking at the two of them put another funny feeling in Sean's chest. This was what he wanted. A beautiful woman in his life and in his bed. A special woman to cherish and grow old with. Children to love and raise the best he could. The kind of life his parents had always said, had proved through living it, was the most important thing in the world. That his dad had wanted him to experience, too.

The kind of life Bree did not want.

He rubbed his hand over his face. Tried hard to remind himself it was Bree's right to have a perspective on life he just didn't understand, and never would. Tried to remember it was important for her to follow her own path when it had become clear hers and his diverged in a way that left a relationship between the two of them hopeless.

Of course it was fine for a woman, or a man, to not want children. He'd tried hard to respect that, but in the end, had to respect himself, too. It wasn't wrong to want children any more than it was wrong to not want that. He'd figured Bree would change her mind, and told her so. She'd accused him of wanting her to be someone different than who she was, and he couldn't deny that was probably true, when it came to that one thing. Otherwise? She was perfection in human form.

When she'd tossed the ring he'd given her back in his face, as much as it had hurt, as much as he'd still loved her, he'd told himself it was for the best. Their differences had gotten more and more obvious, until the child conversations had been the final straw that had broken the engagement.

Leaving him bleeding.

As he watched her sleep, he felt a little like that now. As if some part of his insides would be slipping away with her when she left. He stared at her beautiful lips, parted slightly in sleep. Moved his gaze to the bruise he should be used to by now. That still made his gut tense when he looked at it.

Maybe she sensed him watching her, because she suddenly stirred, looking as if she was going to roll over onto Will. Sean's hand shot out to keep her in place, but she stilled before he touched her. Her hand lifted, fluttered as though looking for something, before it lowered softly onto the baby's tiny body. Almost as though she knew, even in her sleep, that he was there. He let the feelings wash over him, the longing and sadness and regret, and wished he could take a picture of her so sweetly touching the baby. Show her that, inside, maybe she did have the soft maternal instinct she claimed she couldn't have and didn't want. Then told himself he was being stupid. That it would be like trying to convince someone who hated their job that they'd love it if they just tried.

Still, he watched the two of them sleep. Wanted to lie there forever, pretending this could be his life, until his watch chimed that it was time for Bree to go to work soon. The clock was striking, and she'd be running out the door without leaving even a shoe behind, just the memories of her he'd never forget.

He exhaled slowly, lifted his hand then hesitated, not wanting to ruin the picture before him. Finally ran his fingers up her soft cheek to cup it in his palm. "Bree. Wake up. It's seven."

She made a little sound that reminded him of last night and his body began to stir again. He leaned over to press his mouth softly to hers, kissing her awake, because it might be the last time he could. The thought tightened his throat, and he had to swallow hard before he tried to talk. "Bree. It's time for you to go to the hospital."

Her eyelids flickered and she blinked at him as he studied the color of her eyes. Committing each gold and brown fleck within that beautiful green to memory. "What time is it?" she murmured.

"Seven. Your shift starts at eight, right?"

She stretched her arms above her head, arching her back, and the outline of her breasts pressed against the sheet as she did. It just about took more willpower than Sean had in his possession to not pull that sheet down and enjoy their sweetness for breakfast.

"I'm not working. I didn't know what all would be going on with your mom last night, so I found someone to fill in for me, since you're working today."

He stared at her. Bree, calling off work for the whole day? "Well. That's really nice of you. But it so happens that I took the day off, too. Not knowing what would be going on with Mom."

"Well," she echoed, a small smile curving her lips. "How about that."

The way she was looking at him sent him reaching for the top of the sheet after all. Why should he resist, if neither of them had to be at work, and he'd enjoyed kissing and touching them half the night last night anyway, with those memories humming in the air between them?

He inched the sheet down, exposing the rosy tips of her breasts. Ran his fingers across them as they instantly peaked in response.

"In case you haven't noticed, there's someone in this bed with us," she said, a half smile on her parted lips. But she kept her arms above her head. Her breasts were rising and falling as she breathed faster, and her eyes were looking at him in a way that tightened his groin and obliterated any and all worries.

"Don't think he'll notice if I do this." He slid the sheet farther down and followed it with his mouth. Kissing and licking her breasts, her flat stomach. Laving her navel until she wriggled and laughed. The laugh turning to a soft moan when he kept going, pushing her thighs apart. Moved to kiss her there, too, and the scent of her robbed him of breath all over again. Robbed him of strength, because she was made for him. Damn it, she was.

But just before his mouth could connect with her sweetness, a short whimper he didn't think came from Bree morphed into a full-fledged wail. He lifted his head to stare at the distraught baby, then at a laughing Bree. "What the heck? Did he have a bad dream, or something?"

"I don't know—do babies dream?" she said. Sean reached to pick the kid up before his red face exploded. "He sure went from sleeping to freaked out in about a nanosecond."

They both grinned at the decibel of noise that could come from such a tiny being. Sean put his knuckle in the kid's mouth and he went to town, sucking on it as if he were chewing on a steak.

"Good thing he doesn't have any teeth, yet," Bree said, "or you'd be bleeding by now."

"Maybe he's not human and eats flesh." Sean cocked his head at the baby. "Right now, the way his hair is sticking straight up off his head, he looks a little like a dark-haired baby orangutan."

"Orangutans are vegetarian, with a few insects thrown in. Not flesh-eaters."

"An alien, then. After all, Emma never would tell us who Will's father is." And in spite of his joke, that reality still ticked him off. He had hopes he or his mother could squeeze it out of her one of these days.

"You've been watching too many sci-fi movies." Bree shook her head, but her eyes sparkled. "And free-spirited though Emma is, I doubt she'd get involved with an alien."

"Yeah, well, with Emma, you never know."

Bree kept smiling as she shook her head again, but Sean's amusement faded as he thought about spending this day with Bree for the last time. He didn't have to think for more than a second to know how he'd like to spend it. Other than in bed with her, that was.

"I've barely seen the sun for about two weeks," Sean said. And wouldn't that have been incomprehensible when he and Bree were together? The surf and sand were two of her favorite things. He'd been a favorite thing back then, too, and his chest tightened with emotion. But she was here with him now, and it was too late to try to protect his heart anymore. "What do you say we hit the beach for a few hours?"

"What would we do with Will?"

"Take him. Don't worry. I know how to pack all the stuff he needs, now." He stuck the baby in the curve of his arm and smiled at the brown eyes staring up at him expectantly, his lips making adorable little Os as he kicked his feet, as if he was excited about something. "Look at him—he seems to know he's about to go on an adventure, doesn't he?"

Bree leaned over to look at the baby. "Gotta say, I think that might just be another burp coming on. But we can pretend he's excited if you want to."

Her green eyes met his with a teasing smile, and his smile back started deep inside before it even formed on his lips, accompanied by that ache he felt every time he was around her. He knew, though, that the ache would be there regardless. A whole day with her would be like a painkiller, getting rid of it short term until it came back in spades later. Being with her had been like a drug anyway, hadn't it? He'd take it until there was none left.

His free hand reached for hers. "How about showing Will how an international surf champion does it, Dr. Donovan?"

Her hand took his, and as their eyes met, he could tell she was feeling the same mixed emotions. "You've got some good moves of your own, Dr. Latham. He's a lucky boy to have an uncle like you teaching him all you have to share."

He nearly blurted that he wanted to keep sharing it with her, but managed to keep his mouth closed.

"I'll get dressed and pack a lunch for us," she said. He watched her slip from the bed in all her naked glory, and it was a good thing he had Will in his arm, or he'd have pulled her back to bed with no chance of seeing the sun that day after all.

"And I'll put him in his seat and grab the surf stuff."

He let himself keep watching her as she moved to the bathroom. The long line of her spine, her skin smooth over the perfection of her toned body, her athletic rear swaying slightly as she walked. Nothing shy about his

Bree, which was one of the many things he'd loved about her.

The thought stabbed, and he closed his eyes for a second. Emma was probably right. If he didn't start dating again sometime fairly soon, he might find himself single forever.

The question was, how could anyone else begin to measure up to Bree Donovan?

He shook off the melancholy that threatened to ruin the day, which he couldn't let happen. He wanted his last hours with her to be another good memory to carry with him forever. "Wilson, today the sack's not going to cut it. Real clothes for a beach day, and an umbrella for your car seat. Are you in?"

The child blinked, which he took as an affirmative. He got the boy ready, pulled all his stuff together, then sat him by Bree's feet in the kitchen as she put together sandwiches. His chest kept filling with an odd happiness, considering everything. As if he were living his dream, and it was real. For this one day, at least, he had everything he'd ever wanted. "I'm going to get the wet suits and surfboards."

"I checked, and the water temperature's seventy today, so we won't need the suits." She looked up at him with a question in her eyes. Maybe accompanied by a little frown. "You don't have one that would fit me anyway. Do you?"

Was she asking if he'd been seeing anyone else? A horrible part of him wanted to lie. To say, *I have a suit that'll fit you*, in a voice that would imply it without actually saying it. To make her jealous. To make her feel bad she'd broken up with him. But that would be childish, and also wouldn't accomplish a thing except to drive a wedge between them, which was the last thing he wanted. "You left one of your older suits here. I didn't bother calling you about it because I knew it was one you wouldn't want back."

"Oh." She turned back to the sandwiches, focusing pretty fiercely on folding turkey slices. "I'm almost done. I'll watch the baby while you get the boards."

It seemed to take a lot longer to get rolling than it usually did. He finally slid into the driver's seat and looked over at Bree as she clipped her seat belt. "How could the addition of one baby create three times more work?"

He watched her turn to him and open her lips, then close them. Shrug. "Mystery of life."

He hadn't thought about how his words had been part of her many arguments about the reasons why she didn't want kids until he'd opened his mouth. He turned his attention to the road and finally had to ask. "Aren't you going to say it?"

Her green eyes caught his. He couldn't read what all was inside them, but she didn't pretend to not know what he meant. "There's no point," she said quietly. "Even if one of us changed our minds on the having-kids issue, there are other reasons it didn't work out."

At that moment, he had a hard time conjuring the reasons. What had they been again? He almost asked, but reminded himself the day was about fun and not conflict.

Hauling all their gear and Will, they walked up the boardwalk to a good surf spot, then climbed over the seawall to set up the blanket and umbrella, putting the baby in his car seat beneath its shade. "I'll stay here with Will while you surf," he said.

"Okay. I'll go get a few. Then it'll be your turn."

"Looks like there are some big rip currents today, so be careful," he said as she took the board. And, yeah, it was a stupid thing to say, since she'd surfed more hours than he could imagine, in a lot more treacherous places than San Diego, but he couldn't help himself.

"I'll be careful." Her smile said she knew what he was thinking, and, because she was confident Bree, didn't need to call him out on that, either. She went on tiptoe to give him a lingering kiss, and his arms wrapped around her, held her close until she drew back, their eyes meeting in a long connection as silence stretched between them. Finally, she turned and he dropped his arms from her body, but kept his eyes on her as she picked up her board and headed to the surf.

He sat next to Will as the pleasure of the day drifted through him. The baby started making little smacking noises and yips, and Sean looked down at him, assuming that meant he must be hungry. But if he was, why wasn't he doing his usual fussing? Maybe he hadn't cried because, tiny though he was, Will liked being on the beach. He was a Latham, after all, wasn't he? As for him, Sean was enjoying it more than he had in a long time, and he knew part of it was his heightened awareness of the sensory sensations. The briny scent of the air, the rhythmic sound of the surf, the feel of the breeze and the heat of the sun on his skin.

The vision of Bree Donovan in a bikini.

Yes, he'd enjoyed her nakedness just hours ago, but seeing her in a swimsuit was an entirely different kind of pleasure. He'd gotten to enjoy that vision briefly on the bay, her body partly covered with a baby. But today there was no such barrier, and he watched her wade through the water much the same way he'd watched her walk into the bathroom. Not much equaled the pleasure of watching her gracefully maneuver a surfboard through the waves, and he felt that same bittersweetness fill his chest.

He sat there half under the umbrella, feeding Will his bottle with the sun burning his shoulder, and let himself soak in the sensations. Thinking about how Bree had felt in his arms. Her kisses. Her touch. The joy and the ache.

How was he going to get over wanting this every day? Just being with beautiful, amazing Bree. Having her beside him. In his life forever. To kiss and touch and make love with. To watch her surf, or work, or make sandwiches, or whatever—it didn't matter. The woman excelled at everything, demanded it of herself, which made mere mortals like him stand in awe. Demanded too much of herself, really, but she didn't believe that.

Sean held the baby closer to his chest, felt his warm little form curling against his bare skin. Bree would be such a wonderful mother, except she didn't want to be. Watching her joy as she jumped off her board, beaming a smile and wave his way before paddling back out to the waves, he knew with certainty any kids would be beyond lucky to have her share her shimmering inner joy with them.

Maybe that was enough. Maybe she'd share that joy with children, like Will, who weren't her own, but who could benefit from who she was when she spent time with them. Maybe achieving her goals, living her life with those accomplishments in mind, were simply who she was. And he was who he was. The end.

"Oh, my gosh, he's so adorable!"

Sean looked up to see two young women in bikinis drop to their knees in the sand, grinning at Will.

"He's so cute and tiny! How old is he?"

"Six days. I think."

"You're not sure?" They both laughed. "Isn't he yours?"

"No, he's my nephew." The girls scooted closer, touching the baby's head, oohing and aahing, and Sean gave a brief smile. He'd had guy friends tell him that babies and puppies were chick magnets, and here was the proof. Maybe once Bree was gone for good, he'd bring Will to the beach to help him pick up women. Unfortunately, though, pretty as these two were, his gaze moved past them to the woman in a blue bikini stepping off the surfboard. Watched her squeeze water from her hair, then tuck the board under her arm to head their way.

With her tanned limbs glistening from the water and droplets cascading down her taut belly, she looked more like a swimsuit model than a caring doctor. A smart, talented athlete who was pure eye candy, too? No wonder the woman was regularly featured in surf magazines.

Even if he'd known how things would turn out between them, there was no way he could have kept from falling for her. Had known from almost the instant he'd met her that he was standing at the epicenter of a coming earthquake, and there was nothing he could do to escape it.

The joy he'd seen on her face was gone, replaced by an odd expression, and it suddenly struck him that maybe she was none too happy that two half-naked young women were kneeling so close to him their breasts were about to touch his arm and shoulder. Well, well. Bree, jealous? It didn't change anything between them, but he couldn't help but feel good about that, anyway, even though that was pretty lame of him.

He turned to the girls, trying to come up with some conversation to prolong the moment. "You like babies?"

"*Love* babies!" one gushed.

"Who doesn't? I can't wait till I have one someday."

He looked up at Bree as she came to a stop in front of the beach blanket to see how she'd react to this statement. Her jaw had clamped shut and her eyes were sparking like the green flash of San Diego lore that could sometimes be seen on the ocean's horizon at sunset. "Your turn, Sean. I'll take Will."

She leaned down, her breasts practically in Sean's face as she snatched the baby up, and he wanted to pull her into his lap as she did. The part of him twisting all around with different emotions nearly told her not to because babies weren't her thing, but how peevish would that be? She'd taken care of the child every bit as much as he had this past week.

She sat on the blanket next to him, cuddling the lucky baby against her breasts, and the girls clearly took this as a hint they should disappear. His arm wrapped around her cool, damp shoulders before he'd even thought about it. "You look good out there, Bree. Wish I could come see you compete in Honolulu next week."

"Me, too." Her lashes were stuck together with salt

water, and the green gaze studying him seemed somber. The irritation or jealousy or whatever had been there melted away into the same sadness and longing that kept overpowering him.

He pressed his mouth to hers. Soft and slow. Wanting to feel the connection between them that, for this moment at least, filled every empty hole that had been gouged in his heart since she'd thrown the ring back at him. "You taste salty," he whispered.

"And you taste sweet. Maybe together we're like one of those energy bars they sell."

He smiled against her mouth. "Maybe. Any idea how we should use our energy?"

"Several good ideas come to mind. How about—"

A small fist flew up between them, giving Sean an uppercut that was so startling, he actually reeled back from it.

"Did that hurt?" she asked, laughing as she kissed Will on the top of his head before jiggling him, since he was squirming around. "Maybe he's going to be a prizefighter."

"I hope not. That's a stiff punch he's got there already. I—"

He stopped talking because Bree had quickly turned her head away from him. He could feel her stiffen as she stared intently at the water. He followed her gaze to see the lifeguard taking big leaps over the waves, carrying an orange rescue can in her hand. Looked beyond to see a bobbing head far out in the water, past what Bree always called the kill zone of the biggest waves boogie boarders and surfers looked for. Farther out than a swimmer would normally be.

He and Bree looked at each other at the same time. "Rip current took him, don't you think? I hope he knows to let it take him north until he's out of it," she said.

"Yeah." They both turned to the water again, and he heard Bree exclaim and point at the exact same time he saw it, too. A second head, about the same distance out as the other, and this person seemed to be working way too hard to fight the current.

He stood. "This isn't good. That one guy is going to exhaust himself, and there's no way the lifeguard's going to be able to help both of them. I'll be back."

She stood, too, clutching Will and staring at Sean, her face etched with worry, but she gave a quick nod. "Be careful."

He mimicked the lifeguard's movements, taking big leaping strides over the waves until it was too deep to do that, then swimming hard. He could feel the rip in the sand making the water pull him out, which wasn't normally a good thing, but in this instance it was. Getting to one of the struggling swimmers as fast as possible might be critical. People unfamiliar with riptides typically fought hard to get back into shore, but, with the water sucking them back out, it was a battle even the strongest swimmer wasn't likely to win.

He saw the lifeguard helping the first swimmer, which he could now see was a woman. "Hey, I'm here to help," he shouted, pausing and pointing for just a second to let the lifeguard know. "I'll get the other one."

She gave him a thumbs-up as she held the swimmer in her arm and let the waves take them up the beach just a bit, away from the rip so they could swim back to shore. Sean focused on the other swimmer. He looked like a fairly big guy, and he was flailing now, starting to go under each wave longer every time.

Sean kicked harder and grabbed the man from the back, wrapping his arms around the guy's barrel chest, hoping he didn't freak out and start flailing around, dragging both of them under. "I've got you. Relax."

The guy didn't react. Didn't fight him or the waves, and for a split second Sean was relieved. Then realized it was because he'd fallen unconscious just seconds after Sean grabbed him.

Gritting his teeth with impatience, he had to let the tide take them just a bit farther before he knew for sure they were out of the rip and he'd be able to swim to shore. He held the guy against his chest and, heading backward, kicked as hard as he could to get to shore, which seemed to take forever. Finally, he hit shallow enough water to drag the man to the beach, lay him on his back and administer CPR if it was necessary.

With the shallow waves gently lapping against the prone guy's sides, Sean stuck his ear next to the man's mouth to see if he could feel any air coming out, and saw the shapely legs of Bree Donovan, and Will in his seat by her side.

"Is he breathing?"

"Can't tell." He pressed his fingers against the guy's pulse. "Don't think there's a pulse."

"The lifeguard truck's driving up the beach, so they know he needs help." She quickly squatted down. "Let me open his airway while you do chest compressions."

He watched her tilt the man's jaw back, pinch his nose closed and breathe. Sean started chest compressions, counting out loud to thirty. Then Bree breathed into his mouth again.

Nothing. Her eyes lifted to meet Sean's for a split second, her mouth pressed into a grim line. "Again."

They went through the cycle once more, and Sean was relieved to hear the siren getting close. Except it might be too late. But just as he grimly hoped it wasn't, the man's chest heaved in a shuddering breath before he began to cough.

"Help me roll him. I bet he's going to throw up water," Bree said. They both pushed him to his side, and water spewed from the man's mouth as he coughed and gagged.

Feet ran their way, and the cavalry took over. Bree, cool, competent ER doctor that she was, filled them in as they asked questions of her and the man. He couldn't talk yet, but he was nodding, and Sean was filled with the kind of exhilaration he didn't get to feel too often as a surgeon. Yes, he had emergency surgeries that saved people's lives, but this? Pulling the guy out of the water and getting his heart and lungs started again, instantly seeing him alive and awake and functioning? Now, that was a damned good day.

"Dr. Sean Latham is the hero here," he heard Bree say, and looked up from their patient to see her gesturing at him and smiling with the kind of pride and admiration he hadn't seen on her face for a long time. "He swam out to get him out of the rip, brought him back to shore, then did CPR. Pretty darn good for a surgeon used to working in an operating room, don't you think?"

The lifeguards pumped his hand, congratulating and thanking him, and while Sean nodded and smiled, he barely heard it. He kept getting distracted by the woman standing a few feet away. The way her hair, now half dry, curled on the ends, the sunlight making it gleam in rose-gold waves as it fluttered in the breeze. The way her admiring green eyes focused on him. The way her beautiful lips curved into a wide smile.

This would probably be the last time he'd ever see her like this, standing on a beach, which was such a part of who she was. Of her identity. And he was filled with the same kind of pride he could see in her eyes. The same love. Wrong for one another that they were, he knew at that moment he couldn't regret having known her and loved her for a time, because he was richer for it. And when she left he'd accept that pain, because having shared a year of his life with her was worth every second of it.

He picked up Will's carrier in one hand and reached to her with the other. "Let's get packed and Will back to the house."

The ride back felt strained for the first few minutes, until Sean couldn't stand it. He talked about the rescue and the swimmers and the lifeguards, because he wanted to go back to some kind of normalcy between them for their last hours together. Something that felt better than this…this discomfort. This sudden distance, like those first days after the accident, and it struck him how long ago that seemed. Like weeks instead of days, probably because so much had happened. And despite the chaos, he and Bree had fallen into step again, in an odd way. Resuming the rhythm of their former life together, sometimes in sync, and at other times completely out of step, like this moment.

Conversation dried up as Sean stashed away the

equipment and Bree put a tuckered-out Will into bed. When she returned to the kitchen, her backpack was in her hand, and they stood awkwardly staring at one another. "You're working tomorrow, right?" he asked, because he couldn't think of anything else to say.

"Actually, no. It's all been so hectic, I haven't finished up what I need to do to move and get ready for the competition. So I said my goodbyes. I'm done there."

If he thought he'd been aching all day at the thought of her leaving, it was nothing compared to this. A sensation that felt as if all his insides had been sucked out, just like the sand and water pouring through the riptide, leaving unwary victims to drown.

She must have seen it on his face and he tried to turn away, but she reached out and grabbed his hand. Tightened her grip as she stepped in front of him, her expression tense and forlorn and determined all at the same time. "Sean. You know I have to go."

He knew, and yet he didn't, and the question quietly left his lips. "Why?"

"You know why. I'm a competitor. A traveler. I've lived my entire life with a suitcase in one hand and a tennis racket or surfboard in the other. I chose emergency medicine instead of a practice because it works for who I am. For my goals and all the things I've wanted for myself for as long as I can remember."

"And then what? When you're older and not competing in sports anymore?"

"I don't know yet." She looked up at him, her eyes begging him to understand. But he didn't. Didn't understand today any more than he had six months ago.

"There'll be a new adventure. New places to travel. New mountains to climb."

"And that's what you want to be." He stated it flatly, because she'd already told him more times than he'd wanted to hear.

"That's who I am." She stepped close and moved her hands to flatten them against his chest. "I understand that not a lot of people want to live like that. That you like a few vacations here and there, but mostly you're a home-and-hearth kind of man. Want the kind of life you grew up with. But if I didn't have my goals, my competitions, I'd have nothing. Don't you understand that?"

"You'd have me." Saying it laid his heart on the table, but it was already so bruised there was nothing she could do or say to make it hurt worse.

"I'm not enough for you, Sean. I'm not the kind of woman you want. That you need." She slid her arms around his neck and pressed her cheek to his. "I love you. So much. But I've realized our breakup had to happen. If we'd stuck together, soon, you'd get frustrated with my travels, and with me. You'd resent not having kids running around in your backyard. Probably stop traveling with me. Then we'd just be apart half the time anyway. And if I stopped doing the things I need to do, I'd be the one resenting it. Don't you see? It's better for both of us to live our lives the way we want to, fulfill our dreams, and that can't happen if we're together."

He wrapped his arms around her and buried his face in her neck. There wasn't anything to say that hadn't been said too many times already. She'd said she wasn't enough for him? That wasn't it, and she had to know it. The truth was, she didn't believe he was enough for her, and she was probably right. "I love you, too, Bree. So much. You know that. And I wish only the best for you, and that your life gives you everything you want." His throat and heart felt raw as he lifted his head to look at her. "Anything I can do to help you get packed?"

She smiled, but it didn't touch her eyes. "I was about to ask you if I could help with Will another couple days."

"I thought your event was in three days. You can't fly to Hawaii and run straight to the beach with your surfboard, you know." He tried to shove some humor into his voice, but couldn't seem to make it happen.

"There are plenty of competitions ahead of me. I think I'll bow out of this one. Stay until I have to start work, so you can concentrate on getting a nanny for Will and all the nursing care and physical therapy in place for your mom and Emma."

He felt so stunned, he couldn't do more than stare at her for ten long seconds. "You've been training for that thing since before we broke up."

"Yeah, well, things happen. And helping with Will and Emma and your mom is important."

Generous. The woman was so generous, on top of everything else. He wanted to grab her and smash her against his chest and kiss her and tell her how amazing she was. Take her up on her offer and keep her in San Diego for a few more hours. For the rest of his life. But he didn't. Couldn't. Hadn't she just said competing was who she was? Last thing he'd ever want would be to stop her from being that person, because there was no one like her in the entire world.

"Thanks for the offer. But I have a nanny lined up already. We'll be okay without you." Neither statement was true. He was getting close to finding the right nurse-maid, as soon as Emma met the three he'd narrowed it down to. But the other? Survive, maybe, but he'd never be okay. "I want you to go to Hawaii and knock 'em dead."

"I'll try," she whispered, a sheen of tears in her beautiful eyes. "I'll do my best to win it for all the Lathams I love."

She cupped his face in her hands and gave him the sweetest, most emotional kiss of his life. When she pulled away, he yanked her back and kissed her long and hard until he finally had to let her go. She turned to grab her backpack, and without another word she was gone.

CHAPTER TEN

"Oh, I've just been dying to come back to Hawaii again!" Marcia Donovan exclaimed as she shoved a straw hat with a pink hibiscus pinned to it onto her head and perched in one of the beach chairs lined up to watch the surf competition. "I'm so excited that you've moved here and plan to compete more often. It's a dream come true for me."

Bree nearly asked why her mother's dreams were always based on Bree's goals and plans instead of coming up with her own, but closed her lips again. Hadn't she promised herself she'd be more understanding of her mother's love for her, even if it bordered on obsession? "I'm glad you're having fun. And it's going to be good to have you help me get my stuff together in the apartment. Probably would have been half together for a long time if I'd had to do it all myself."

"I still don't understand why you're starting work as soon as you're scheduled to, but you never listen to me anyway." The smile on her face took any annoyance out of the words. "What number are you again?"

"Seven." Bree squinted at the other competitors congregating at the shoreline. "Speaking of which, I need to get over there. See you after, okay?"

She positioned her board under her arm and got in the queue, her belly feeling a little strange. There was always an element of nerves and tenseness before a big event like this, but somehow that didn't seem to be it. And as she looked around at all the people clustered as far as she could see on the beach, it struck her exactly what it was.

Sean wasn't there. For the first time since they'd started dating, there was no tall, handsome man standing in the crowd, the sun glinting off his chestnut hair, giving her a thumbs-up over everyone's head. Flashing a big, proud smile and pumping his fist after a good run. And despite the thousands of people on the sand, the beach felt strangely empty.

She turned to study the waves, analyzing how they were breaking, but kept seeing Sean instead. Yes, she'd been in a dozen or so events in California since their breakup, but they'd all been small and more of a training session for Bree than a real competition. But this one was big-time. A major surf event televised around the world.

Would he be watching from his living room? From the doctors' lounge at the hospital? Would he want to see her compete, or try, instead, to forget all about her as soon as he could? Probably forget her, and still following her second career of surfing wouldn't be the best way to make that happen. He deserved the kind of woman he wanted. The kind of woman Bree just wasn't capable of being.

A child shrieked in delight and she turned again to

look at the masses gathered on the beach. Old and young, couples and families. A woman stood holding a baby just a month or so older than Will, and a pang of emotion stabbed her chest that she wasn't going to get to see him grow up, though of course that was silly. She could visit Emma anytime she wanted, except that might open up the awful possibility of seeing Sean with a new girlfriend on his arm. Maybe even a wife and child of his own.

She drew in a deep breath of salty air and watched the first surfer head into the water. Tried hard to concentrate on the event. Thought about her dad, and how he'd texted her earlier that he'd be watching, and how much she'd love to hold that winning trophy up high for all the world to see. Thought about how great that felt when she was able to make that happen. Thought again about tiny Will, and how she'd like to teach him to surf someday, and how he might be impressed with those trophies the way other people often were, enough to actually listen.

She knew those moments would be few and far between, living so far away. Which was a good thing, even though it didn't feel like it right then. As she headed into the water, she found she was picturing Will's little face and Sean's smile, and somehow both helped her focus on what she had to do to tackle the giant waves in front of her. Do what she'd trained to do.

Which was win.

Sean stared at the television image as he absently patted the baby on his shoulder, barely noticing the short but loud burp in his ear.

"That was a good one!" Emma said.

He glanced up to try to focus on his sister, seeing

her pause in her computer search with a wide grin on her face. "Because he takes after you. I remember how you used to burp as loud as possible, and Mom would get mad at you while Dad laughed."

"And I still don't like it," his mother said as she moved slowly down the hallway toward the living room. "Not ladylike at all. Never understood why all the rest of you thought it was so funny."

Emma tried to burp as she had as a teen, and his mom frowned at her instead of getting the joke. She started in again on the importance of being polite and genteel, and Sean had to interrupt if he had any chance of hearing what the commentators were saying on the television. Which then became even more unlikely when Will started crying. "You know, if it weren't for that whole near-death thing for all of you, I'd say this house has gotten awfully loud and crowded," he said.

"You know you love having us here," Emma said with another mischievous grin.

Truthfully, he both did and didn't. He loved all three of them, and was thankful every day that they were still here on Earth. Not to mention he'd hated the horrible, empty quiet when it had been just him all alone after Bree left. But, strangely, even with his house overflowing with family, in some ways it felt lonely anyway. And his sister bugging him about getting back on the dating train and his mother fussing about all kinds of things weren't exactly relaxing, though he wasn't about to complain considering everything.

His attention was caught again by the beautiful surfer with fiery golden hair, maneuvering a thirty-foot wave with the grace of a sleek dolphin born in the sea.

"Sean," his mother said in a gently chiding voice as she took the baby from his arms. "How many times are you going to watch that recording? The competition was over a week ago. Maybe you should just delete it. It's not good for you if you're trying to move on."

Was he trying to move on? He didn't know. All he knew was that he wanted to keep watching Bree on one of her runs, then look at her as she moved onto the beach after each one. Wishing he'd been there to support her, at the same time he knew that was stupid and sad.

"Speaking of moving on, here's another good possibility," Emma said, awkwardly turning the computer screen his direction with the arm she had in a cast. "A schoolteacher—she's really pretty and about your age. Has a little kid, but that's not a problem, right? Since you want a family someday."

He barely glanced at the photo. "She reminds me of Mrs. Simmons, my fourth-grade teacher. Wouldn't work."

"That's been your answer for everyone I've shown you," Emma complained. "Hey, this one might be perfect! She—"

"Just stop!"

His sister and mother stared at him in stunned silence. He hadn't meant to shout it, but enough was enough. "How can you expect me to even look at another woman, when that one—" he jabbed his finger at the TV screen "—that insanely beautiful, talented, incredible woman, told me just last week that she loves me? You don't get over that in a week. Or a month." Or even ever, the way he was feeling right now.

"Then why aren't you with her?"

"Because I'm not who she wants."

"Did she say that?"

All the things they'd said to one another six months ago and last week got jumbled up in his head until it hurt. "She said she's not enough for me."

"Well, if that's true—"

"Of course it's not true!"

"Then I repeat, why aren't you with her, if she thinks the reason you're apart is because she's not enough for you?"

It felt a little as if he'd been hit in the head with an atom bomb. He stared at his sister, then slowly moved his gaze to his mother holding the baby that was continuing the Latham family tree. It struck him that everyone he cared about the most was in this room, except for one person. Bree Donovan. And at that moment, he couldn't even remember all the reasons he and Bree had become convinced they were wrong for one another, because none of them mattered.

The only thing that mattered was that he loved her and she loved him, and if one of them had to give up something they wanted so they could be together, it was going to be him.

"I need to go to Hawaii. Will you two be okay for a few days if I double up on the nursing help?"

"Finally." His sister leaned back in her chair and gave him a slow smile before she started to clap, which didn't make much noise since her cast covered most of her palm. "I was beginning to think setting you up with this dating service wasn't going to work. Took you long enough to admit you're never going to be happy without Bree."

He stared at her. "So bugging me to date someone else was a scheme?"

"Yep. I figured if you went on a few dates, you'd figure out no one would ever measure up to Bree. Thought maybe it would make her jealous, too. I know you two knuckleheads can figure things out if you try."

His mother stood with Will and looked at him. "I've been upset with her for breaking up with you, but if Bree is who makes you happy, I'm all for it, and your father would be, too. Because parents can't stand for their children to be sad. You go. We'll be fine."

He folded her and Will in his arms for a quick hug, moved to kiss Emma's cheek, then got busy. Made a plane reservation, called the hospital to get his schedule moved around, got the extra nursing set up and packed a bag. And every minute that passed sent his adrenaline pumping higher, along with jangling his nerves. What if he'd finally seen what he really wanted, but it was too late? What if she'd moved on, and decided that it was really over between them for good?

He blew out a heavy breath, wishing he'd gotten his head on straight before she'd left. While he'd still had her close, held captive by Will. He walked back into the living room to say goodbye. "My flight leaves at—"

He stopped, then went utterly still when he saw his mom and sister weren't the only people there.

Bree Donovan stood in the center of the room.

He was so shocked to see her, he couldn't react. Couldn't breathe. Just stared. But she had the advantage of knowing he'd be there, and moved toward him.

"Hi, Sean."

"What are you doing here?"

"I need to talk to you. Can we…maybe go outside for a minute?"

All the words he'd rehearsed to say to her when he found her in Hawaii left his head, and he just nodded like an idiot. As they moved toward the front door leading out to the bike path around the bay, he remembered his mother and sister were there as they passed. Both were looking at them with rapt attention, and he picked up the pace so he and Bree could have privacy to talk.

Except he had no idea what she wanted to say, which scared him to death.

He didn't touch her as they walked slowly down the path. Didn't know if he should or shouldn't, and didn't know if he should be the one to start the conversation he'd decided to have with her.

"Bree, I—"

"I came back to San Diego—"

Both stopped talking and chuckled a little nervously. "Okay, you go first," he said.

He saw her draw breath, and she looked down at the path instead of at him, which scared him again. "I came in third at the surf competition."

He didn't know what she was going to say, but hadn't expected a surfing update. "I know. I saw. You were amazing."

She stopped walking. Her head lifted and her serious green gaze met his. "I was really happy with how I did. Lola and Katie got some great waves and just plain out-surfed me. Being in the top three at that level is a big accomplishment, you know? It was good."

"I know."

"So after all the photos and interviews, I looked at my phone. I…I admit I was looking to see if you'd sent me a message."

"I thought maybe you wouldn't want to hear from me. But I couldn't help myself. Watching you surf is… Well, it's like watching moving art. I had to congratulate you."

"It meant a lot to me," she whispered. "All day you not being there with me felt wrong. But along with yours, I had another message. From my dad. And instead of congratulating me like you did, he told me all I'd done wrong, all the reasons I didn't win." She laughed, but there wasn't any amusement in the sound. "He doesn't even surf, but thinks he's an expert. Told me the things I had to do better. And I realized at that moment that no matter what I did, what I accomplished, to him, it would never be enough."

She reached for his hands, and he held hers tight, wondering where she was going with this. Listening, wanting to hear, at the same time anxiety churned in his gut, needing so badly to tell her all he had to say before it might be too late.

"It struck me that I'm not that little girl anymore who wanted to prove to him and everyone else that I'm worth something. You asked me what would come next when I couldn't compete anymore, but I hadn't thought that far ahead. Standing on that beach last week, I realized, finally, that all I want is to be with you. All I need is you. Just you."

He couldn't breathe. He could see the fear in her beautiful eyes as she spoke. The same fear that had filled him, and he cupped her face in his hands the way she had touched his the day she left. "That's a funny thing. Because all I need is you, Bree. That's it. You. I was on my way to Hawaii to tell you that, if you'll have me back, I don't care where we live. A condo by the beach, a big house in the suburbs, it doesn't matter so long as you're in it with me. I wouldn't care what kind of wedding we had, or where we had it. I'll come with you wherever you want to travel, whenever you want, or stay home every day of the year. It's up to you." His chest squeezed tight with emotion and he had to stop to press his lips to her forehead for a second before he could go on.

"I have my mom and Emma, and now little Will. I can be the best uncle in the world, and that'll be enough for me. If you're by my side, that's all I'll need or want for the rest of my life."

"Oh, Sean." Her voice was wobbly and she pulled back to look at him. "I'm still figuring out exactly who I want to be. But there's one thing I don't have to figure out, and that's how much I love you."

He pulled her close and buried his face in her hair, finally able to breathe. They stood holding one another for long minutes before he was able to let her go. Because there was one more thing he had to ask.

"Will you marry me, Bree? I messed it up before, but I hope—"

"Yes, I'll marry you." She gave him a smile so radiant it stole his breath. "But you don't have to buy me a diamond, since I lost the last one. A wedding band to show my forever commitment to you is all I need."

"I wasn't planning to buy you another diamond." He

slipped his hand into his pocket, anticipation welling at how she'd react. "Because I don't have to."

Her mouth fell open in a gasp as he held out the ring. "How did you find it? I looked for it on that stupid street for days!"

"After you stormed off, I went down there. Hoping maybe finding it would be a good omen that you'd someday come back to me. And there it was. Shining gold in the sunlight the way your beautiful hair does." He reached for her hand and slipped it on, and seeing it there again after the long, dark months without her weakened his knees.

He pulled her close for the longest kiss of his life, which slowly morphed from sweet to hot. Then he remembered that his small house was full of people at the moment. "How about we find a hotel room for tonight, hmm?"

She tunneled her hands into his hair, and his knees felt weak all over again that he'd get to look in her eyes every day of his life. "I can sleep on a cot, or the beach, a bed or the floor. It doesn't matter to me. So long as I'm with you."

EPILOGUE

BREE LEAPED OFF her surfboard and scanned the crowd on the beach, elation filling her chest. And despite the thousands of people gathered there cheering, her gaze went straight to what she was looking for.

Her husband. Her family.

Sean couldn't do the thumbs-up or fist pump he always gave her when she'd had a great run because his arms were filled with two ten-month-old babies who were taking over for him. They were waving their pudgy little hands and grinning at her across the sand, the sunlight gleaming on one blond, curly head and the other covered with darker hair like his daddy's.

Bree carried her board over, then dropped it to the beach to reach for one of her babies. Olivia leaned forward first, and Bree took her in her arms, neither caring that she was getting her daughter's clothes a little wet. Jack kept his small arms curled around Sean's neck as his smiling brown eyes met hers over their son's head.

"You looked pretty amazing out there. Your score's going to go through the roof with that one," Sean said.

"I think you're right. I think I just might have a chance to win the whole thing this time."

Sean leaned forward to press his lips to hers. "Mmm. This is my favorite time to kiss you, when you're all salty and sweet."

"And my favorite time to kiss you is anytime."

He chuckled as they smiled at one another, pressing his mouth to hers again until a squirming Olivia knocked her head into Sean's and disrupted the kiss.

"I'll take her for you," Bree's mother said, beaming as she reached for her granddaughter.

Bree passed Olivia over, watching as her mother smiled and cooed and the baby laughed. Having children of her own had brought her closer to her mother as she finally understood the bond between a woman and her child in a way she'd never considered. They had shared a lot of long talks over the past year and their relationship was the best it had ever been.

Jack wriggled in his daddy's arms, and Sean placed him on the sand next to where Will was playing with plastic buckets and shovels. Jack scooped and dumped sand onto Will's knees, which the three-year-old didn't seem to mind at all.

Emma and Gwen both congratulated Bree, too, before they sat in their beach chairs to supervise the little ones, trying to keep the sand from being flung around and ending up in someone's eye.

Sean took advantage of the momentary peace to take Bree's hand and walk a few paces away. His tanned fingers tucked wet strands of hair behind her ears before he cupped her face in his hands, and she leaned into him as he did.

"I'm so proud of you. You worked hard for this."

"I did. But I couldn't have done it without you. Without everything you do, every day, for me and for all of us. I'm the luckiest woman in the world." It was true, and saying it brought a lump to her throat, because even after all this time, she hadn't forgotten how close she'd come to losing him forever. To not having the amazingly full life she was blessed to live every day.

"And I'm the luckiest guy." He kissed her again, his hands moving from her face to her back, pulling her close.

"I think there's something you want that will make you even more lucky, and I'd like to give it to you."

"Yeah?" She loved the wicked glint that sparked in his eyes. "I'm all ears. What is it you're going to give me, and how soon do I get it?"

"You'll find out the day after tomorrow."

His eyebrow rose before his lips touched the corner of her mouth and tracked to her ear. "I was hoping to get it before then. Not sure I can wait that long."

"You can't get it till we're back home. Because it's there, not here."

"Obviously this is a different kind of luck than what I was thinking of," he whispered in her ear before pulling back to grin at her. "What is this mystery thing I'm getting from my beautiful wife?"

"That puppy you've been wanting? I found the perfect one at the shelter. We're picking her up on Monday."

"Really? You don't mind our getting a dog?" His eyes lit, and she loved that she could give him one more thing he wanted.

"I'm excited about it. The kids will love her, and

besides, you deserve everything you want. You deserve the moon."

"Thank you. I don't know about deserving anything. But what I do know?" He kissed her again, sweet and slow and perfect. "My everything is you."

* * * * *

If you enjoyed this story, check out these other great reads from Robin Gianna

THE PRINCE AND THE MIDWIFE
HER CHRISTMAS BABY BUMP
HER GREEK DOCTOR'S PROPOSAL
IT HAPPENED IN PARIS...

All available now!

MILLS & BOON®
Hardback – September 2016

ROMANCE

To Blackmail a Di Sione	Rachael Thomas
A Ring for Vincenzo's Heir	Jennie Lucas
Demetriou Demands His Child	Kate Hewitt
Trapped by Vialli's Vows	Chantelle Shaw
The Sheikh's Baby Scandal	Carol Marinelli
Defying the Billionaire's Command	Michelle Conder
The Secret Beneath the Veil	Dani Collins
The Mistress That Tamed De Santis	Natalie Anderson
Stepping into the Prince's World	Marion Lennox
Unveiling the Bridesmaid	Jessica Gilmore
The CEO's Surprise Family	Teresa Carpenter
The Billionaire from Her Past	Leah Ashton
A Daddy for Her Daughter	Tina Beckett
Reunited with His Runaway Bride	Robin Gianna
Rescued by Dr Rafe	Annie Claydon
Saved by the Single Dad	Annie Claydon
Sizzling Nights with Dr Off-Limits	Janice Lynn
Seven Nights with Her Ex	Louisa Heaton
The Boss's Baby Arrangement	Catherine Mann
Billionaire Boss, M.D.	Olivia Gates

0816 GEN STD HB

MILLS & BOON®
Large Print – September 2016

ROMANCE

Morelli's Mistress	Anne Mather
A Tycoon to Be Reckoned With	Julia James
Billionaire Without a Past	Carol Marinelli
The Shock Cassano Baby	Andie Brock
The Most Scandalous Ravensdale	Melanie Milburne
The Sheikh's Last Mistress	Rachael Thomas
Claiming the Royal Innocent	Jennifer Hayward
The Billionaire Who Saw Her Beauty	Rebecca Winters
In the Boss's Castle	Jessica Gilmore
One Week with the French Tycoon	Christy McKellen
Rafael's Contract Bride	Nina Milne

HISTORICAL

In Bed with the Duke	Annie Burrows
More Than a Lover	Ann Lethbridge
Playing the Duke's Mistress	Eliza Redgold
The Blacksmith's Wife	Elisabeth Hobbes
That Despicable Rogue	Virginia Heath

MEDICAL

The Socialite's Secret	Carol Marinelli
London's Most Eligible Doctor	Annie O'Neil
Saving Maddie's Baby	Marion Lennox
A Sheikh to Capture Her Heart	Meredith Webber
Breaking All Their Rules	Sue MacKay
One Life-Changing Night	Louisa Heaton

816 GEN STD LP

MILLS & BOON®
Hardback – October 2016

ROMANCE

The Return of the Di Sione Wife	Caitlin Crews
Baby of His Revenge	Jennie Lucas
The Spaniard's Pregnant Bride	Maisey Yates
A Cinderella for the Greek	Julia James
Married for the Tycoon's Empire	Abby Green
Indebted to Moreno	Kate Walker
A Deal with Alejandro	Maya Blake
Surrendering to the Italian's Command	Kim Lawrence
Surrendering to the Italian's Command	Kim Lawrence
A Mistletoe Kiss with the Boss	Susan Meier
A Countess for Christmas	Christy McKellen
Her Festive Baby Bombshell	Jennifer Faye
The Unexpected Holiday Gift	Sophie Pembroke
Waking Up to Dr Gorgeous	Emily Forbes
Swept Away by the Seductive Stranger	Amy Andrews
One Kiss in Tokyo...	Scarlet Wilson
The Courage to Love Her Army Doc	Karin Baine
Reawakened by the Surgeon's Touch	Jennifer Taylor
Second Chance with Lord Branscombe	Joanna Neil
The Pregnancy Proposition	Andrea Laurence
His Illegitimate Heir	Sarah M. Anderson

MILLS & BOON®
Large Print – October 2016

ROMANCE

Wallflower, Widow...Wife!	Ann Lethbridge
Bought for the Greek's Revenge	Lynne Graham
An Heir to Make a Marriage	Abby Green
The Greek's Nine-Month Redemption	Maisey Yates
Expecting a Royal Scandal	Caitlin Crews
Return of the Untamed Billionaire	Carol Marinelli
Signed Over to Santino	Maya Blake
Wedded, Bedded, Betrayed	Michelle Smart
The Greek's Nine-Month Surprise	Jennifer Faye
A Baby to Save Their Marriage	Scarlet Wilson
Stranded with Her Rescuer	Nikki Logan
Expecting the Fellani Heir	Lucy Gordon

HISTORICAL

The Many Sins of Cris de Feaux	Louise Allen
Scandal at the Midsummer Ball	Marguerite Kaye & Bronwyn Scott
Marriage Made in Hope	Sophia James
The Highland Laird's Bride	Nicole Locke
An Unsuitable Duchess	Laurie Benson

MEDICAL

Seduced by the Heart Surgeon	Carol Marinelli
Falling for the Single Dad	Emily Forbes
The Fling That Changed Everything	Alison Roberts
A Child to Open Their Hearts	Marion Lennox
The Greek Doctor's Secret Son	Jennifer Taylor
Caught in a Storm of Passion	Lucy Ryder

916 GEN STD LP

MILLS & BOON®

Why shop at millsandboon.co.uk?

Each year, thousands of romance readers find their perfect read at millsandboon.co.uk. That's because we're passionate about bringing you the very best romantic fiction. Here are some of the advantages of shopping at www.millsandboon.co.uk:

* **Get new books first**—you'll be able to buy your favourite books one month before they hit the shops

* **Get exclusive discounts**—you'll also be able to buy our specially created monthly collections, with up to 50% off the RRP

* **Find your favourite authors**—latest news, interviews and new releases for all your favourite authors and series on our website, plus ideas for what to try next

* **Join in**—once you've bought your favourite books, don't forget to register with us to rate, review and join in the discussions

Visit **www.millsandboon.co.uk**
for all this and more today!